TRUTH SEEKER

A DREAM WEAVERS & TRUTH SEEKERS
NOVELLA

CECILIA DOMINIC

Dear Morgan,
I hope you enjoy
four good truths!

Truth Seeker

ISBN: 978-1-945074-45-5

Edited by Holly Atkinson

Cover art by Kiersten Fay

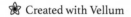 Created with Vellum

PART I

THE TUNNELS

1

---

ny second now...

Phillippe's watch had stopped fifteen coffee shops ago. One of those "atomic clock" things that re-set itself according to time zone, it had given up. He hoped it wouldn't detonate in a mini mushroom cloud on his wrist.

He slouched in his chair, his back against the display case of blue and silver coffee and travel mugs. Snow swirled outside the window and obscured what he assumed was the business district of a medium to large city. He would have preferred to sit in a warm corner away from the window, but at this point information equaled survival.

In spite of his annoyance, he willed the muscles in his face to be pleasantly neutral. He didn't want to draw any more attention than he already did with his lack of overcoat and snow boots. Maybe people would think he came from some northern clime where people were more accustomed to the cold. He wore his black tennis shoes, blue jeans, green T-shirt, and open flannel under a blue denim jacket. Philippe, just as glad he wouldn't have to go outside, wondered what *she* would wear this time. The only constants in her wardrobe were colored lenses and all black clothing. He had never seen her eyes without the glasses.

No matter what jump he made, she always arrived twenty minutes after him. They never spoke or acknowledged each other's existence, but she always gave him a clue as to where he was. He guessed that he was in Ohio or north-central Kentucky from the assortment of Cincinnati, Cleveland, and Kentucky papers left at the front or on the tables. That would fit with the weather and the neutral Midwest accents.

He thought about the chart he'd made on the back of a napkin of all the places he'd been since he'd stumbled into this unique mode of travel. What had begun as an accident was now a game of cat and mouse, and Philippe imagined the jaws of the trap as they closed a little more each time he used the tunnels. He wasn't sure that *they* knew who he was, and he had no clue about *their* identity. His one certainty was that he hadn't been back to his origin point. Now he wanted to solve the puzzle so he could bail out somewhere close to home in the Northwest.

He glanced at his watch, remembered it didn't work, and looked at the clock. Any second now...

The door opened with a whoosh of cold air, and *she* walked in. Philippe's resolve cracked, and he smiled at her windblown beauty. Her long, thick strawberry blond hair hung straight and breeze-tousled below her black beret, and blue-tinted lenses partially hid her eyes. He sat straighter as she studied the pastries. He knew every one of them intimately by now, but he didn't dare make a recommendation. She waited for the portly lady in front of her to pay for a hot tea and scone and ordered a tall nonfat latte. The barista told her the total.

"$2.55, please. Are you having a good day?"

"I am, thank you." She smiled. "Everyone seems so friendly here in Cincinnati."

Philippe snuck his napkin out and made a notation—he'd been right.

The barista returned the girl's smile. "We have our meanies, but in general, yes, we're pretty nice."

Philippe studied his makeshift map, unable to discern a pattern. The locations ranged from small towns to large metropolises. He rarely landed in the same state twice a day, and he never left the shops for fear that he would be stranded.

The air changed—a low hum that he felt in his bones from his jaw to his tailbone to his feet. Time to go. The sensation propelled him out of his chair. He threw away his white cardboard cup and folded the newspaper he'd left at his table. On a whim, he took out his pen and scrawled a note on a paper napkin, which he dropped by the spiked wooden heel of the redheaded woman's left boot as he walked past.

The storeroom of the coffee shop was located off a small hallway. Philippe wondered if he would ever be able to tolerate the smell of coffee beans again after he got out of this mess. Burlap sacks lined the walls of the small closet, regular to the right, decaf to the left, and espresso in the back. One of them glowed a warm mocha, the aroma of coffee translated to a visual sensation. He looked over his shoulder one more time and touched the rough burlap sack.

The glow moved up his arm—a warm, electric tingle and all his hairs stood on end. The room receded into a dark brown fog, the bag melting away under his pinching fingers. He peered into the tunnels, a series of hallways diffused with coffee-colored light. His footsteps made no sound as he ran down the hall, the sense of someone after him even stronger this time. There was one door, which he yanked open. He could almost feel the breath of his pursuer on his neck as he tumbled out on to the burlap sacks, and he finally felt he could exhale without someone hearing him.

He pictured himself as a rodent who crept through the

shadows of that strange world, glimpsed in the peripheral vision, but gone before seen.

This new closet opened on to a long, red-tiled hallway. He made sure no one was around, then slipped out and turned to the left. What luck—restrooms! The ones in the last place had been outside the store, which he'd been afraid to leave. He went into the men's room and stood at a urinal. A young man in a suit came in with a wheeled carry-on and laptop case. Philippe looked away. Two more men came in, both with luggage, and a middle-aged guy with a little boy. The kid pulled a miniature red and yellow wheeled carry-on behind him.

Philippe exited the bathroom and the hallway to find ticket counters. This was his first airport stop, and he noted that on his napkin. Security guards patrolled the checkpoint and kept watch at strategic intervals. For the first time in days, Philippe felt safe, and he didn't even need the redhead to tell him where he was this time. A sign over the exit blinked, "Welcome to San Antonio!"

He pondered his options. He didn't make enough money at his waiter day job or cover band night job to pay for an airline ticket home. With a thrill, he wondered if the redhead had read his note or if she'd even noticed it. He strolled into the coffee-shop to wait. Sleep deprivation made him incautious, and he forgot to order something before he sat down.

"The seating area is for patrons only, sir," one of the baristas snapped.

"I'm waiting for a friend."

Philippe studied his list. Downtown Cincinnati to the San Antonio Airport. Even though he hadn't had a choice, he felt pleased. At least it was warm here. He imagined what it would be like to just walk outside, catch a shuttle to the Riverwalk, and have some real food and a margarita. He guessed this place would be open all night, or at least most of it, and he could sneak back into the closet whenever it called to him. He hoped.

"You're getting careless, Philippe."

He jumped up and found himself face-to-face with the redhead. She wore the same all-back outfit as in Cincinnati, except she carried the sweater and wore a black spaghetti-strap top under the leather jacket. This time her sunglasses had light purple lenses. She tossed his note on the table, and his scrawl mocked him with what must have seemed desperate words —*Talk to me, please – Philippe.*

"Now that we've met, I can buy you a cup of coffee," he offered.

"You've been traversing the tunnels for four days now." She looked at him, and he realized how disheveled he must appear. "Allow me to buy you dinner."

Four burritos, a margarita, and a chalupa later, Philippe was ready to talk. The woman, who had introduced herself as "Margaret, but everyone calls me Maggie. Don't even think of calling me Mags," sat across from him and picked at her taco salad. He'd panicked for a moment when they left the airport and the coffee shop—was he shutting himself off from his only route home?—but he sensed he could trust her.

"You've hardly touched your sangria," Philippe said. Or thought he did. The earth tilted, and his tongue felt loose in his head. He'd been stupid to order the margarita, but he needed to unwind.

"I'm not supposed to drink on the job." She smiled. "But you can. First question: how did you end up in the tunnels?"

Philippe wished he could make full eye contact, but even though they sat in shadow, she wore her purple lenses.

"A couple of my buddies and me went for coffee after work on Monday," he explained. "One of them, Arnie, dared me to slip past the baristas into the back and snitch some beans."

Maggie raised an eyebrow.

"Childish, I know." His cheeks heated. "I went, but someone came in behind me, so I looked for a place to hide. I ducked into the closet and decided, while I was in there, to just grab some beans from one of the sacks." He paused and tried to figure out how to explain what had happened next.

"Go on." She leaned forward.

"I found one with a little hole in it, and then this warm tingly feeling washed up my arm, and then, whoosh, I was in this place full of tunnels and doors." He watched her. Was she buying it?

She looked over her glasses at him.

What the hell? Her eyes were yellow. No, gold.

"What happened then?"

He had to keep going. The words spilled from him before he could help it. "I freaked out and opened the first door I came to. Let me tell you, I was surprised as hell to find myself in someplace with palm trees."

Maggie pushed her glasses up her nose. "Sorry, they slip. Go on."

Maybe he'd been so sleep-deprived he'd dreamed up her weird eyes. They looked normal now. "So then I took a few minutes to get my bearings and figure out where I was by looking at the papers. Tampa, Florida. Across the freakin' country." Now he looked at her to make sure she didn't think he was nuts.

"That's not surprising. Go on."

"Well, then a bus full of old people pulled up, and they stampeded inside, so I took the chance to go back to the storeroom and try to find my way back. This time I saw the bag glow, so I touched it, and zap! Back in the tunnels."

"Did you have any idea what you needed to do to get back?"

Philippe shook his head. "I just kept trying, figuring that I would get to the right one eventually."

"Your friends are really worried about you." She leaned back and studied him with crossed arms. "When you didn't reappear from the back, they told the baristas, who looked for you. A day later, you were listed as a missing person. A buddy of mine at the police station saw how you'd disappeared and gave me a call."

"Are you the coffee police?"

Maggie chuckled, a sound like wind-chimes. "Hardly. I've been trying to get into those tunnels for almost a year now. I even took a job as a barista, but I got fired for some spurious reason."

He knew how that went. "So what do you have to do with all this if you're not the one who built the tunnels?"

"I'm afraid I can't divulge that right now. Let's just say that my organization is not the only one that's very interested in you."

Philippe's heart thudded, although her statement confirmed what he'd sensed. "Me? Why?"

"You're the first unauthorized breach of the tunnels, and the builders, and whoever's behind them, are panicking. They would like to interrogate you, I'm sure."

"I have some questions for them." Philippe's face flushed. "They had no right to keep me from getting home."

"And if they caught you, they'd kill you, so being trapped away from home is the least of your worries." She fiddled with her napkin and spoke in a low, intense tone. "It's how they think, Philippe. They consider you to be equivalent to an animal, like a research rat who's escaped. They figured that if they kept you running scared and away from home, they could catch up to you. Luckily I did first."

He checked to find the nearest exit. "What do *you* want with me?"

"I want to know everything in the smallest detail, what the tunnels are like, how you get in them, how you get out, and how they work. I want to know who built them, what their purpose is, and how to destroy them."

"You're a lady with a lot of questions." Philippe yawned. "Can we talk about this later? I've been running on caffeine and sugar for the past four days."

Maggie nodded, pulled a black leather wallet out of her jacket, and laid down enough cash to cover the meals and leave a tip. She stood and gestured for him to do likewise.

"I have a good friend here. We can stay with him. If anyone asks, we'll tell them you're my boyfriend."

She turned, and Philippe studied her slender back and nice ass. "No problem."

Rat or no, he liked this maze.

2

———

Maggie made sure Philippe was safe in his bedroom over the inner courtyard of the hacienda. She took her glasses off, rubbed her eyes, and caught her reflection in a mirror. Without the colored lenses, her eyes shone yellow-gold. No human could lie to her upon direct eye contact, but they rarely stuck around long enough for her to ask the questions. Sometimes she longed for the old days when spirits had been respected as well as feared. Modern mortals who had lost touch with their spiritual side tended to faint or flee when she revealed herself.

"All asleep, Mags?" Raphael, one of the few men who had never shied from her, smiled at her from the top of the stairs, his face a mask of wrinkles.

"You know you're the only one who can call me that." She grinned back. "He slumbers peacefully. I'm sure he's exhausted."

"Come down and have a cup of coffee. I know you don't need sleep, but it may perk you up, no pun intended."

Maggie followed him down the stairs through the lobby and to the kitchen. The whole place, an old hacienda turned resort ranch, was decorated in desert pastels, golden wood, and native American-inspired patterns on the walls and furniture. She put her lenses on so mortal guests would assume she had nothing more remarkable than sensitive eyes. She changed the appearance of her garments so that she wore a black sundress and sandals.

Raphael Angeli, the owner and proprietor, gestured for her to have a seat behind the counter that separated the kitchen from the dining room. He poured two cups of coffee and set one in front of her.

"Cream? Sugar?"

"Yes."

Raphael smiled. "Impertinent girl."

"I'm hundreds of years older than you, old boy."

"True enough. So that's the mortal you've been chasing?"

"Yes." She fixed her coffee with just a little sugar and a lot of cream. Raphael knew how she took it, but she feared his memory was slipping. The mortals' minds all did after a time. "I'm just as happy to have caught up with him here. At least my vacation wasn't interrupted too badly."

"You know you've always got a room here, spirit-girl, even after your reservation ends. All you have to do is ask."

"I'll put in a good word for you with your namesake." Maggie put a freckled, unwrinkled hand over his gnarled, knotted fingers. "You're a good sort for a mortal, Raph."

"I'll never forget the first time you came through here." The old man smiled at the memory. "I was seventeen, and you were the most beautiful thing I'd ever seen, especially with those gold eyes of yours."

Maggie laughed and shook her head. "That you fell in love with a Truth Seeker at that age says a lot about your integrity, Raph. Teenagers tend to be deceptive creatures."

"And young men." Raphael gestured in the direction of Philippe's room. Then his expression turned serious. "Is that why you didn't reciprocate? You know I didn't care—don't care—what you are."

Maggie stirred the beverage in front of her even though it didn't need any more mixing. She'd trusted Raph with a lot, but not with her greatest vulnerability.

"You can tell me," he insisted. "You know I can keep a secret."

She wondered what it would be like to unburden herself. But what if it made him feel more attached to her? It could put him in greater danger, more than he was already in.

"Let's just say it never ends well when mortals love someone like me."

"Because you outlive us?"

Good, he'd gone for the obvious explanation, and she hadn't had to lie, only misdirect. "Something like that."

"What about that one?" He inclined his head toward the building where Philippe slept.

"Raph, we've only just met." She admitted to herself Philippe had a nice bad boy look about him, but his story had told her he lacked maturity. Or was she just too old and tired? That he'd been able to go into the tunnels held a certain intrigue.

Raphael brought her out of her thoughts. "Do you think he can be trusted?"

She smiled at the old man's protectiveness. "I have difficulty feeling that one out. There's something about him..."

"Uh oh, you sound like someone who's about to fall in love."

Maggie shook her head. "He's just another one in a long string of mortals I have to deal with. I don't think I'll ever find another like you, Raph."

Now Raphael placed his hand over hers. "You could retire, you know. Settle down. I'm too old to make you happy, but someone like your friend there..."

Maggie laughed and looked away. "You know I can't lie, so I'll admit it's tempting to retire and settle down."

"You've been alone a long time."

"Ages. But I've got too much work to do. There's bad magic afoot."

He nodded, his expression serious again. "Someone's up to mischief for sure, then?"

Maggie glanced at the sky. A gray cloud had come over the sun, shadowing the entire area. "Something like that. I can't believe that whoever it is has managed to build this network right under our noses. The chain's fairy logo should have tipped us off that a nonhuman is involved."

"You've been busy for the past few years." Raphael patted her hand. "Even immortals make mistakes when they're overworked."

"I'm just concerned that it's gotten this far." Maggie gestured to Philippe's list, which he had given her upon request. It started in the Northwest and spanned all parts of the country. "Some powerful spirit is building a fast transportation network, and I still don't know who intends to use it...or for what."

"More coffee?"

"Please." Maggie sat back in her chair and pondered the list. "And can anyone use it? That's the big question. The trick is in finding the right bag at the right time. Something causes the beans to charge on a spiritual level, but the phenomenon doesn't happen all the time."

"And he just stumbled on it?" Raphael shook his head as he poured the steaming black liquid into the cobalt blue mug. "I don't believe in coincidence, Maggie."

"Coincidence doesn't believe much in humans, either. I'll send her with her sister Dumb Luck for a visit sometime, and you can change each other's minds."

"He's involved somehow, mark my words, girl. He may be the key, even if he doesn't realize it." Raphael looked straight in her golden eyes. "You may have to truth-spell him."

"I know, but I hate doing it. My glasses slipped, and I accidentally did a little at dinner."

"I know you hate it. That's why you're the Truth Seeker."

"The job's up for grabs if you want it."

Raphael laughed, his teeth large in his wrinkled face. "I'm too old to learn to be an immortal. I'll leave that up to you."

"Thanks."

"Though you could use a partner."

Maggie arched an eyebrow. "Thanks, but I work best alone."

"Just a thought from an old man's wandering mind. How long are you going to let the boy sleep?"

"As long as he needs. *I* feel worn out after chasing him, and I don't require slumber. He must be exhausted."

"Go for a walk, then, and puzzle it over. I'll call you when dinner's ready."

MAGGIE HEADED west through the scrub. To her, the place seemed crowded, even though there weren't many mortals in the off-season. She nodded to the spirits she saw and waved to the familiar ones. Raphael's ranch was a healing place for some, a haunting place for many. And he welcomed them all. His kind soul had been one reason she'd opened up to him decades ago. And his shamanic heritage had allowed him to see what she was. She'd miss him when he went on, and guessed he'd be called to a greater plane than an earthly haunting.

The spirits seemed restless. Sometimes her presence alone unsettled them, as though they felt that one of the law enforcers of the spirit world was a threat. She ignored it as usual and just enjoyed being outside. She could feel warm if she wanted to, but she didn't bother with mortal sensations. What haunted her was not current events or even the mystery of the coffee shop chain, but Philippe's dark eyes. Mortals often fell in love with her, but she rarely felt anything in return. She'd thought it carelessness that he trusted her, but she realized that he sensed something of who she was, although like most mortals, he'd gotten it wrong. He considered her his traveling muse, his guide.

And he'd been hell to catch. But she had caught him. She always did.

Maggie watched the sun set, then turned back toward the ranch. A dark cloud seemed to hang over the buildings. Not wasting time with walking, Maggie zapped herself straight back to Philippe's room, where he still slept, but twitched. She slipped through the door to the hallway just as Raphael ran up the stairs.

"What's wrong?"

Raphael, his tan face ashen, clutched his chest and spoke in gasps. "Vampire bats. A whole horde of them nesting in the trees."

"They didn't hurt you, did they?"

"No." Raphael struggled to catch his breath. "But they say they'll swarm if we don't hand over the boy."

"Oh, for Pete's sake. Seriously, are you okay?"

He nodded. "Just winded. I don't move as fast as I used to. But where are they coming from, Maggie? There's too many of them to be from around here."

The potential explanation chilled her. "Maybe they traveled the tunnels."

"Can you zap you and him out of here?"

Maggie shook her head. "Too risky. If I lose my hold on him, he'd be doomed to tumble through nonspace forever."

The sound of leathery wings and claws on wooden shutters startled them.

"You'll have to risk it. Once full dark settles, who knows what they'll do to the humans here?"

Maggie studied Raphael with a frown. "Are you okay? You don't look well."

Raphael shoved her back toward Philippe's room with surprising strength for his frail appearance. "You take the boy and go. I'll be fine."

The thought of losing the target she'd worked so hard to catch made her hesitate. "I guess I don't have a choice."

"There's always a choice, girl."

Maggie went into the room, where Philippe, his eyes wide with fright at the squealing and clawing at the windows, sat up in the bed.

"C'mon, kid, we're out of here."

"Kid?" Philippe smiled at her. "You can't be that much older than I am."

"You have no idea. Now take my hands." She held hers out to him.

"Wait. Let me put my shoes on."

"Hurry!" The shutters sounded like they would rattle off at any moment. Philippe slipped his feet into his sneakers without tying them.

"That'll have to do. Now." She grabbed both his hands, yanked him off the bed, and thought about where she wanted to go. Someplace far away and too small for one of those large chain coffee shops...

THE BATS BROKE through the window, a black cloud among splinters of wood, and Philippe ducked before the image faded and blurred into dark colors that resolved themselves into the main street of a small town. The ground under his feet tilted— a sidewalk on a hill. They stood on the corner of the business district, and a blinking red light illuminated the storefronts in flashes. Maggie held his hands so hard it hurt.

"You can let go now." As soon as he said it, he wished he hadn't.

She cocked her head before releasing him. "Are you all the way here?"

"I think so." He tried to shake the feeling back into his fingertips. He could see his breath and cursed that he was underdressed for the weather...again.

"We need to get you a coat," Maggie told him. "And some new shoes. You lost one."

Philippe looked down. His small toe peeked out of a hole in his left sock, and his foot grew numb with cold. His face heated again. Something about her made him feel like all his secrets were exposed.

"Hmm..." All of the businesses had "closed" signs in the windows. Philippe sighed and hoped he wouldn't have to walk all the way to one of those 24-hour places.

"Got any friends here?" he asked.

"As a matter of fact, I think I do. Let's see if he still answers his old summons." Maggie walked over to the glass front door of the nearest store. The town must be tiny—none of the shops had bars over the windows. Maggie blew on the glass to fog it, then drew a symbol on it and muttered something in a language Philippe didn't recognize.

In a moment, a tall gentleman in black appeared and enveloped Maggie in a hug.

"Margaret, how good of you to come." The man's accent said South. Deep South. "What brings you to Salisbury?"

"I need a favor, Beauregard. We're on the run, and my friend here is freezing and has lost a shoe."

"And he's hungry, too, I imagine." The man's gaze pierced Philippe to his marrow, and Philippe shivered harder as the ghost's eyebrows raised.

Maggie grinned, and Philippe tried to feel as unperturbed as she seemed. "You were always the gentleman."

"I was, wasn't I?" He smiled, but Philippe shivered harder. Beauregard looked half-ghoul, half-funeral director. "Now that

I'm retired, I don't have access to as many resources, but I think I may have something that will do."

Beauregard led them down the main street, up a hill, and through an old neighborhood in the revitalization process. As with many Southern towns, some of the homes had just been renovated and were inhabited, while others stood empty. Philippe sighed with relief when Beauregard stopped in front of one of the empty ones. He knew he could see his two supernatural guides, but he didn't know if anyone else could.

Not that it mattered; the entire town was asleep.

"Isn't this your old house, Beau?" Maggie peered through the diamond panes of the front door. "Very nice. When do the mortals move in?"

"In two weeks. After the hardwood floors are put in."

Philippe looked around. Red brick with white columns and a wrap-around porch, the old house whispered to Philippe of hoop skirts and iced tea on the verandah at noon. He could see shadows of its life, ruin, and rebirth in the windows, and his extra way of seeing reminded him of what had drawn him to the magic coffee bag. While he'd always been able to see shadows of the past, his talent had never led him into trouble. Until now. But he also thanked his ability for introducing him to Maggie, who fascinated him more with every word and strange deed.

The lock snapped back. Beauregard opened the door and gestured with one long, white hand for them to precede him inside. They walked into a front hall with a chandelier and grand staircase. The huge front room, empty except for piles of hardwood flooring, echoed with their footsteps. Philippe was relieved to be enveloped in relatively warm air, and his ears tingled.

"Are you warming up?" Beau asked Philippe.

"Yes."

"Good. I believe the clothing of which I'm thinking is in the attic."

They climbed the stairs, and Beauregard led them to the left to a narrow door. He opened it, and Philippe sneezed at the musty smell which emanated from the small, unfinished staircase.

"This leads upstairs, where it is still quite chilly. You may stay here with Margaret, and I'll find some suitable attire for you."

"I'll come," Maggie volunteered.

"No, my dear, you would get in the way. I'll only be a moment."

Philippe and Maggie sat on the top step of the main staircase and looked down over the hall.

"Are you okay?" Maggie asked him.

Philippe wished she would take his hand again. "I guess." He looked at her. "Do you trust this guy?"

Maggie nodded. "Beau and I are old friends."

"Creepy friend."

"It's his job. He's a ghost."

"A house as old as this should have some ghosts," Philippe agreed to counter the defensiveness in her voice.

She relaxed her shoulders and smiled. "Beauregard was part of my organization, but retired a couple hundred years ago, lived out a mortal life, and decided to stay on as one of the town's haunts."

"The only haunt of any quality in this area, I might add." Beauregard handed him a long wool coat and a sturdy pair of boots.

Philippe put them on. They fit perfectly.

"What about food for our young friend, Margaret?"

"Of course. Back in a flash." She disappeared, and the light in the hall seemed to dim.

Philippe looked at Beauregard, who gestured for him to

follow and said,"You may spend the night in the attic. With the coat and some blankets, you should be quite comfortable."

"Didn't you just say it was chilly?"

"Did I? Why don't you come see for yourself?"

Beauregard led Philippe up the narrow stairs, which creaked and popped. Philippe's heart pounded, but not from exertion, and he glanced over his shoulder.

"What is she?" he asked to distract himself from the uneasy tickle in the pit of his stomach.

"What are you? What am I? We are but a collection of energy, some more dense than others."

Philippe found a seat on an old chest and looked up at Beauregard.

"Your feelings for her demonstrate integrity on your part, my young friend."

"What feelings?"

Beauregard smiled, his lips stretched thin over his teeth. "Pursuit is futile, you know."

The wind howled and crept through the gaps in the insulation, and the air crackled with electricity. Philippe shivered. "Not to seem ungrateful, but is there another place I could sleep? It's cold."

Beau seemed to ignore him. "Have you ever seen what the mortals nowadays call 'thunder-snow?'"

What did that have to do with anything? Could ghosts get dementia? Something was definitely off about Beauregard. Philippe stood and edged toward the stairs. "No. We mostly get rain where I'm from."

"It's quite a spectacle. The lightning flashes green because of an abundance of a certain element in the air. I wish I could explain better, but my scientific training ended with Newton."

Lightning flashed outside, but green instead of white. Beauregard glowed for a few seconds after, like he'd gathered the energy. Philippe wished Maggie would return.

"You never answered my question," he told Beauregard through chattering teeth.

"Which one?"

"Any of them."

Beauregard moved almost too quickly to see and blocked Philippe from the stairs. "Perhaps you should ask a question that matters."

Philippe balled his fists but remembered he couldn't punch the ghost, who would probably turn transparent when he tried "Those matter to me."

"And you matter, young man." Beauregard turned his intense gazed at Philippe. A shot of adrenaline raced through Philippe's body, and he struggled to catch a breath.

"Why?"

"That is a good question."

"That's not a good answer."

Beauregard moved closer. Philippe backed against the wall.

"How did you get into the tunnels?"

"How did you know about that?" His heart pounded at his throat, but he couldn't see an escape route.

"Knowledge for some is a lifelong quest."

The next flash of lightning outlined the silver buttons on Beauregard's black coat.

"But for most, it is a fool's errand because they do not know what they truly seek."

Icy talons grasped Philippe's left wrist, and he was flung against a burlap bag filled with beans that, when crushed, released a familiar aroma. The same energy as before gathered in the bag, but his entire awareness focused on Beauregard's fangs and forked red tongue, which hovered inches from his jugular vein.

"Stimulating, isn't it?" Beauregard licked the air by Philippe's ear. "That aroma. I hope you'll forgive me. I like a little blood in my coffee."

"Stop!" Maggie hurled the fast-food bag she'd carried up the stairs at Beauregard's head. He put up a hand to block it, and Maggie took hold of Philippe's right arm, starting an awkward game of tug-of-war. Philippe clenched his left fist and twisted hard. Beauregard's grip slipped, and with a clap of thunder, Philippe and Maggie stood outside with wet snow on their faces.

3

"What the hell was that?" Philippe tried to look into Maggie's eyes, but she dropped her gaze. "Betrayal. Lies. And I didn't see them."

She trembled, and Philippe put his other arm around her and pulled her close into a hug. She stiffened but didn't pull away.

"I'm so sorry, Philippe."

She looked up at him for the first time without her glasses. They lay at her feet as snow filmed over the broken lenses. Her tear-filled eyes glowed golden in the dark. As Philippe looked into them, he saw that she told him the truth. He resisted the smile that tried to curl the corner of his lips. She'd made a mistake; that made her human after all. Well, mostly. And her eyes... An irresistible urge to tell her everything he'd ever done, good and bad, built at the base of his tongue, and he opened his mouth.

"Don't." She put a hand over his lips. "I don't need to know everything."

She looked down, and the flood of words stalled. He choked out, "Hey, we all screw up sometimes."

She shook her head, her hair a veil on either side of her face. "Not like this. I almost handed you right over to them, whoever they are."

"So sometimes you can't tell who your friends are. It happens."

"I should be able to tell." She tried to turn away, but he pulled her closer.

"You should always be right?"

"I'm the Truth Seeker, Philippe." Her fists hit his chest. "I should know!"

Philippe recalled how he felt when he realized he couldn't get back home in the tunnels. "Hey," he murmured and tucked a finger under her chin to bring her gaze back to his eyes. "Everyone makes mistakes. And uncertainty makes life interesting."

"Or frightening," she whispered. This time she didn't resist when he hugged her. She even tucked her hands inside his coat. They stood for a few minutes, and he held her while she cried.

Maybe Truth Seekers, whatever they were, needed to be taken care of, too. He'd ask her more about what exactly she was when they were someplace warmer.

"I'm okay now." She pulled back and wiped the tears off her cheeks with the heel of her hand. Philippe wrapped his coat around him to keep the warm spot where she'd been. She bent over to search for her glasses.

"Who could have turned Beau?" she asked. "He was one of our best."

"People change."

"Not Truth Seekers..." She shook her head. "No, it couldn't be."

"What?"

"It would have to be someone quite powerful. But her?"

"Who, her?"

"I think we have some questions to ask." She looked up at him and smiled. "And I think we're in the right place to ask them."

"Where are we?" Philippe looked through the swirling snow to see if he could figure it out.

"Boston, in the middle of the Commons. If it wasn't snowing so hard, you could see the statue up there." She gestured up a little rise.

"I've never been here." His face heated again. She'd obviously been all over the world, at least the country, and as for him... Well, he had barely been out of state until this misadventure.

"The Yankee ghosts are the worst gossips. If there's something going on, we'll find out here. Aha." She found her glasses and shook the snow off them. She put them on, and they came back together in green lenses as her garments changed to reflect the weather: long, sturdy leather coat, black boots and jeans, and a soft black hat with a rim that folded back up. "Do I look mortal again?"

"You'll never look mortal to me." Philippe's romantic statement was ruined when his stomach growled.

Maggie giggled. "You're probably starving. I could use a bite myself."

"Surely in a big city like this, there are some all-night joints."

"Coffee?" She grinned.

"What else? Wait." He looked around, but all he could see was swirling snow. "Someplace local, right?"

Maggie nodded and stepped beside him to put a hand on his biceps. "I think I know a place around here..." She sniffed the air. "That way."

She led him through the calf-high snow to an asphalt path. They followed through the park to a street that, even at this time of night, was crowded with traffic. Philippe squirmed inside with pleasure at the pressure of her hand on his arm. He had known several women through his career as the guitarist for a cover band, but he'd never found one so hard to understand. Of course, this was no ordinary woman.

"What about here?" Her voice brought him out of his daydreams. "They have bagels, too."

"A bagel would be perfect."

They walked past a flour truck, its thick hose extended into the basement, and a fine film covered their black.

"Drat, my new old clothes." Philippe pretended to be disgruntled as he brushed flour off his coat.

Maggie cocked her head and looked up at him. "They suit you. You were born a century too late, I think."

"Or several," Philippe wanted to say, but was interrupted by a barked, "Whaddaya want?" from a man in shirtsleeves behind the counter.

Maggie gestured for Philippe to order first. After the man grumbled through pouring their coffee and assembling their bagels, they took a booth by the window.

At first Philippe turned his full concentration to his wheat bagel with sun-dried tomato cream cheese, but once he'd satisfied the edge of his hunger, he noticed that Maggie nodded and gestured to an empty table.

"What are you doing?" Philippe hissed. He glanced at the bagel assembler, who ignored them. When he looked back and reminded himself to use his extra vision, he could see a transparent young woman in revolutionary-era dress. He groaned. The last think he wanted at this point was to see another ghost.

"Friend of yours?" he whispered.

"Who can tell anymore?" Maggie shrugged. "But yes, an old acquaintance."

The ghost glided to their table and slid onto the booth beside Maggie. Her form, shadowy and translucent, appeared fuzzy around the edges, but Philippe could tell that she had been very pretty during life with large, dark, almond-shaped eyes set in an oval face with a pointed chin. Blond curls peeked out from under her starched white cap.

"What brings a Truth Seeker to Boston?" Her voice, shadowy like her form, seemed almost a whisper. "We have had no spiritual crime."

Philippe wanted to ask what brought a ghost to a bagel shop, but a look from Maggie stopped him.

"I'm not here to track any of the locals, Betsy," Maggie said.

The ghost seemed nervous, but she looked young. She couldn't have been more than fifteen or sixteen when she died. She smiled.

"Then welcome to you and your handsome friend." Philippe blushed and hoped that was a little flush that crept on to Maggie's face as well. "But there are better cups of coffee in town, you know."

"Oh?" Maggie asked.

"There's the place of the fairy that seems to attract the mortals in droves." She gave a sharp nod and a sigh. "Aye, nobody here drinks tea anymore, and it's such a part of our history."

Maggie glanced at Philippe, and he read the question in her face: could this one be part of the conspiracy, too?

Betsy stiffened. "If you think I've turned traitor," she huffed, "allow me to remind you that I was one of the first Revolutionaries. I would not give up my liberty for anything."

"We never said anything about traitors," Maggie reminded her. "Tell me what you know."

"I know that since the accursed place opened its doors, I've not seen my brother James for more than two seconds at a time."

"I think I remember him." Maggie frowned. "Killed in the same blast that got you, maybe a couple of years older?"

"Aye, as if that matters once you've reached two hundred." Betsy snorted, and Philippe hid a grin. The girl had spirit, no pun intended. "He tried to get me to join, too, but I had my hotel circuit to keep me busy."

"Hotel circuit?" Philippe's curiosity got the better of him.

"Betsy is one of Boston's most famous ghosts," Maggie explained. "She appears at hotels in the area where her house was."

"It's honest work for a ghost," Betsy added.

"Wait, I've heard that before." Maggie took off her glasses. Betsy shrieked and started to disappear, but Maggie pointed a finger at her and held her where she sat. The Truth Seeker looked deep into Betsy's eyes. Betsy shuddered and moaned. Maggie put her finger down and replaced her glasses. Betsy slumped in the chair.

"You know I hate that, Margaret."

"Sorry, Betsy, it had to be done. We've already been betrayed once." Maggie looked tired, too. "Why did you fight so hard? You're an honest little spirit with nothing to hide."

"It's a person's right to resist interrogation if they haven't been accused of a crime."

Philippe coughed to hide a laugh, but Maggie grinned.

Betsy pouted. "If you want to know what it's all about, you can talk to James. I can take you to him."

"It sounds like another trap," Philippe pointed out.

Maggie nodded, but Betsy shook her head. "He'd never betray me."

"Are you up for it?" Maggie asked Philippe. "You must be exhausted."

"That's the best part about living in the Pacific Northwest— you get used to running on caffeine in the dark."

MAGGIE AND PHILIPPE followed Betsy down the main street and through some narrower side thoroughfares until they stood in front of Phanuel Hall.

"This is James' haunt," Betsy explained.

"He must be moving up." Maggie looked around. "The last time I was here, he was a dock ghost."

Philippe smirked—everyone had a hierarchy—and looked around the small square. The squat building in front of them made for quite a contrast with the surrounding high-rises. He jumped as a pale, thin man with the same eyes and hair color as Betsy but with a square, stubborn jaw and a mean mouth, appeared. This glowing ghost seemed more substantial.

Maggie reached for her glasses, but icy hands gripped all of their wrists and held their arms behind them. Philippe looked up and behind him into the cold, black eyes of a redcoat.

"How could you trap us, Betsy?" Maggie wailed, a harrowing, wrathful sound that the wind and snow picked up and carried around them.

"I didn't know." Betsy's cry melted into the wind, and she disappeared.

James pointed at Philippe. "That's the one she wants."

"She who?" asked Maggie. She twisted against her captor, a ragged revolutionary soldier, but he held her firm.

"Not that it's any of your business, golden-eyes, but you'll find out soon enough."

Philippe struggled, but his captor wouldn't let him wriggle off.

"I had no idea ghosts could be so substantial," Philippe told Maggie as they were marched past the hall, down an alley, and into the back room of one of the chain coffee shops. The door wasn't open, which wasn't a problem, as Maggie and her escort passed right through it, but Philippe came up hard against it as his guard stumbled and went through him and the door. He hesitated—what about Maggie?—but he heard her shout, "Run, Philippe!"

4

The boots, although heavy, gave Philippe excellent traction in the snow. The cold air burned his nose, throat, and lungs, but he sprinted back the way they had come. Something cold pressed at his back, and he darted up and down random streets to shake it, but it seemed to follow him no matter where he went.

As he approached a bed and breakfast, he saw Betsy pop out of a side door and beckon to him. He made a quick right and half-ran, half-tripped through a doorway that a brown-haired young man held open for him.

After Philippe landed on the floor, panting, he looked up into the face of his savior and saw that the youth, another ghost, had been burned on one side of his face so that one of his green eyes was closed and the dark brown hair had been singed off. Then the wound healed in front of Philippe's eyes, and the ghost, who had been a handsome young man, winked.

"Stop showing off, Thomas," Betsy scolded.

"How did you get them to stop chasing me?" Philippe looked back at the door as though they would tumble in after him at any moment.

Betsy looked at Thomas, who nodded. "Immortals, like mortals, have places where all but those who are invited are forbidden," she explained. "Only the most powerful spirits can make such determinations."

"You're not just playing with ghosts and Truth Seekers, my friend," Thomas added. "Your situation is of interest to those all the way up the ladder."

"There's someone else here," Philippe looked around at the dark timber walls of what he now perceived was a store-room, but although no noise came to his ears, he sensed the presence of another being, like a weight above them.

Thomas smiled. "You do have some talent. This was my guardian's house, and he keeps himself well-hidden and unable to be detected by ghost-hunters."

"Stop teasing him, Thomas." Betsy gestured for Philippe to get up and follow her, and Thomas helped him to his feet with icy hands. The expression on Thomas' face as he looked at Betsy sent a pang through Philippe.

Was he so obvious when he looked at Maggie? How could he have left her in such danger?

"She'll be fine," Thomas assured him. "Sorry to intrude on your thoughts, but your worry came through your fingers."

"We hope," Betsy retorted. "No one is supposed to be able to hurt a Truth Seeker, but they were able to restrain her, which is unheard of." Her heels clicked against the hardwood floor in an angry staccato. "That someone would do such a thing... And that James would use me like that." She shook her head. "I'm so mad I could be a poltergeist. No offense, Thomas."

"None taken." Thomas seemed more amused than offended.

"Do we not have standards anymore?" She sniffed. "If mother were a ghost... Oh, I'd've liked to have seen what she would have done to him. Taken a lick out of his hide, that's what."

"She gets like this when she's mad," Thomas explained to

Philippe with a twinkle in his green eyes. His shaggy dark hair flopped in his face, and he swept it back with a hand covered in gold rings. He dressed in a more exotic manner than the other spirits, in rust-colored breeches with buckled shoes and a loose-fitting silk shirt.

Philippe's curiosity got the best of him. "Do you mind if I ask where you came from?"

Thomas wiggled his fingers, and his jewels flashed. "Not at all. My guardian and I were smugglers. When the British set up a blockade, we ran it to deliver rum and sugar to the colonists. We were caught and both died under house arrest here."

"Killed yourselves, you mean," Betsy admonished. "At least admit you didn't die an honest death."

"Well, we can't all be lucky enough to be blown up by the enemy. What the authorities would have done to us was much worse than what we did to ourselves. Took the gentleman's way out, we did."

"And your wound?" Philippe asked.

"We burned ourselves alive." Thomas dropped his voice as they reached a door. "They took all our weapons."

"What's all this clatter?" A gruff voice with a British accent growled at them from the other side of the door. "D'you have the boy?"

"Aye, sir." Thomas opened the door, entered the shadowy room, and bowed. Betsy curtsied. Philippe wondered if he should do something and started to bow, but a laugh startled him.

"Act according to the manners of your time, young man. Come give me a hearty handshake."

Philippe advanced with an outstretched hand, but gasped and snatched it back when a metal hook at the end of a black velvet sleeve came out of the shadows. More laughter.

"Just kidding, lad. We spirits don't have nearly enough chances for fun."

The hook faded and was replaced by a tanned hand. Philippe shook it. And tried not to react to its cold clamminess.

"I like a warm handshake, lad. Sorry if you do. Can't help the conditions beyond the grave, you know."

Philippe attempted a smile and sat in the chair the hand waved him to. It then drew back into the shadows. Philippe tried to see what, or who, sat there, but all he could make out were twin points of light where eyes would be.

"I apologize for not showing my face, but I haven't yet caught on to young Tom's trick of transforming it, so mortals find me gruesome. Most immortals, too, truth be told. Young Betsy can't stand to be in the same room with me for too long. But she keeps coming back. 'Tis amazing what love will do."

Philippe glanced back, and Thomas dropped Betsy's hand.

"Get along with you, young'uns. Give the lad and me some privacy."

"Yes, Rothfeather," Thomas said before he and and Betsy disappeared. The ghost in the shadows sighed.

"I apologize for the rudeness. When we're with mortals, rare though it is, I tell them to act as they do and walk in and out of rooms like polite spirits. Just disappearing like common ghosts..." Metal clinked as the old smuggler shook his head.

Philippe continued to gaze at the twin points of light as they moved from side to side. They stopped and returned his stare. He looked away.

"I like a man who makes eye contact, even with someone who doesn't have eyes."

"I wish my gaze was as talented as Maggie's, sir. Not that I distrust you..." But not even his second sight showed him anything.

"You should, lad. You should be suspicious of all of us, except for that redheaded gal. That one can't lie. A rare treat in a woman, that." A third gleam appeared beneath the other two —a grin with a gold tooth?

"How am I going to rescue her?"

"That one can take care of herself." But Philippe heard the same note of doubt that he'd heard in Thomas' voice.

Rothfeather's statement sparked a question.

"What is she? I mean, what is a Truth Seeker?" Philippe asked.

"They're a supernatural law-enforcement agency. Or at least they fancy themselves as such. Can't lie. Or not supposed to, anyway." A flash of gold in the shadows told Philippe that Roth-feather waved away his curiosity – mostly. "There are more important issues to discuss, lad. Related issues."

Maggie was a cop? He should've known—it all clicked into place when he thought about it, which he couldn't help. Nor could he prevent the pang of disappointment that she hadn't originally come looking for him specifically. Philippe shifted his weight—regardless of who or what she was, she had risked her life for him, and he had to do something for her, not have a long discussion with a ghost who had all the time in the world. But if he was to have help, he needed to go along with the discussion. Hopefully related issues wouldn't take too long.

"I do have some questions."

"As I do for you." The spirit settled back in his chair. "How long have you been able to see ghosts?"

Philippe tried not to show his impatience. What the hell did that have to do with anything? "It's hard to explain. Before it was just shadows, shapes in the corner of my eye. But since I've been in the tunnels..." Philippe shrugged. "I can see them very clearly now, especially when I'm with Maggie." Worry twisted in his gut. She'd shown him a layer to the world he'd never suspected. And gotten trapped by it.

"An honest answer. We'll get along fine, you and I. Next question: how did you end up in the tunnels?"

Philippe told the old pirate the same story he'd related to

Maggie, but a shorter version. The pinpoints of light moved up and down as the ghost nodded.

"You probably felt a compulsion, as they like to say, to go in that store-room, didn't you?" Philippe nodded, and the spirit when on, "Only one with talent could do that. There are a few in each generation. My Tom was one of them. That's why, even after death, he can affect the world of the living."

"You mean, as a poltergeist?"

"That's it, lad. Every generation of the living produces those who can communicate with the ones on the 'other side,' as your television personalities like to call it. Some make money speaking to departed loved ones, some go insane, or think they do because they see and hear things that others don't. And some, like you, stumble into it by accident."

Philippe felt that there should be more. "And...?"

"What do you know about ghosts?"

Another question. Philippe stifled a sigh. "They're human spirits, souls, I guess, who got stuck here after being separated from their bodies. Maybe a violent death tied them to a certain area like you, Tom, and Betsy... Maybe they have something left to do..." He stopped. "I guess I don't know as much as I thought I did."

"I'll tell you three things that you have to remember, Philippe. First, those that stick around aren't happy because one needs an earthly body to enjoy earthly pleasures. Second, they're so jealous of humans for what they have and experience without appreciating it that some of those spirits don't stop at just scaring them."

Philippe shivered as he remembered Beauregard.

"And third, if they could find some way to get past those limitations of being body-less, they would do anything to do so."

Now they were getting to useful intel. "What limitations, besides not being able to eat, drink, and have sex?"

"Being stuck in one place. You've heard all the stuff about not being able to cross water and spiritual boundaries, like those around my house?"

Philippe nodded.

"All are simplifications of the complex rules that govern the afterlife. Most of us can't go beyond a certain radius of where we died. Those that do find that their strength wanes so quickly that they have to return immediately or they're stuck in one place until another spirit comes along and is willing to help."

"So if they could travel through spiritual space rather than physical..."

A terrible thought struck Philippe. The pirate nodded.

"It's the travel, not the distance that wears us. Eliminate the travel, and you'll have spirits joining forces to take over the world from the living."

A chill crept over Philippe from the pit of his stomach outward. "Why are you telling me this?"

"There's a price for your talent, lad. Those that can see spirits are bound by universal law to do something that will benefit them." A disfigured burned face came out of the shadows toward Philippe, bits of charred flesh and hair stuck to its white skull, its blank eye sockets houses of flickering white light. Philippe choked on a scream.

"I caused enough harm during my life," the face said through ragged lips, "that I cannot stand idly by during death. I and all others will have their release from this torment."

"When?"

"I don't know, no one does, but it will happen. But when it does, those who have robbed humans of their rightful life-spans will be doomed. Most think that they can't have it any worse than they do now. I know with certainty that they can. Your task, young man, is to keep that from happening."

As if the task looming ahead wasn't big enough. "How?"

"Find the builders, or, I suspect, builder, of the tunnels.

Destroy what they have constructed." The ghost leaned back into the shadows, and Philippe tried to slow his breathing, but the ghost's next words chilled him. "Before they lure others—human and ghost—to their eternal doom."

HOW IS THIS POSSIBLE?

Maggie strained against her bonds, the discarded cords of religious habits. She knew that some spirits could be restrained by such devices, but she, a Truth Seeker, should be beyond such influence. The authority she wielded was from the highest power. She, too, had a price: a large ransom, but not gold or silver. Her captors bargained for her existence. Even though her body wasn't human, it could be destroyed, and then she would be left like one of them, nothing more than a collection of loose energy trapped on this plane until the end of the world.

"Hello, cousin."

Maggie looked up, and her lips curled in a snarl before she could catch herself.

"Niniane, I suspected it was you."

A tall young woman in a black gossamer gown stood before Maggie. Her golden hair flowed over thin shoulders, and cruel green eyes sparkled with a wrath built over centuries.

That explained the bonds. Niniane had a piece of Maggie's hair, a lock exchanged when they were children. With it, Niniane could wield certain power over Maggie. Margaret, the enchanted sister left out of the King Arthur tales, had joined the Truth Seekers, a society for the search of the elusive Grail of Truth that had developed into a spiritual law-enforcement agency. Niniane, commonly known as the Lady of the Lake, had turned against the knights—and all humans—after Avalon had been destroyed.

As a rule, Maggie let others handle Niniane, but this time,

she had been trapped, her first mistake. Her second was that, although she had a lock of Niniane's hair, she did not keep it with her because its evil energy attenuated her powers. It was well-hidden, true, but still vulnerable and beyond her use.

Niniane gloated. "So I hear you've seen your old colleague Beauregard."

"And noticed that you managed to seduce him into your wild scheme."

"Not so wild. Soon the world will be the property of the fairies, elves, and spirits again. And the silly humans are financing the whole venture."

Niniane twirled something around her finger—the locket with Maggie's hair.

"Yes, I still have this." Niniane dangled it in front of Maggie's nose. "Where's mine?"

"Why do you want to know?"

"It should be obvious. It's the only way I can be stopped—if someone finds it and binds or banishes me."

"It's well hidden." Maggie's heart sank. Yes, she had hidden the locket at Raphael's ranch, but there was no way she could get word to someone to find it—not until it was too late.

"As for your pet... You're improving, Margaret. That one looked like a keeper." Niniane snickered. "That should be him right now."

Light footsteps descended the stairs, and the ancient wooden door to her cell banged open. The two ghosts who had followed Philippe, a redcoat and a colonial soldier, were empty handed.

"Well?" Niniane snapped.

"He got away. He ducked into old Rothfeather's house."

Niniane hissed. "He would choose the home of that burned-up fool."

"James' sister helped him."

"Curse her. Why must I always be foiled by virgins?"

Maggie ducked her head to hide her smirk. She knew Betsy wouldn't let her down.

"I wouldn't smile if I were you, dear Margaret." Niniane's lips parted over pointed teeth. "You may have gotten away with the one mortal who can trespass in my tunnels, but the old man in Texas will, ah, join his more permanent guests soon if you don't tell me where the locket is hidden. Beauregard is on his way there now."

Maggie remembered the ashen pallor of Raphael's skin and wondered if the tall ghoul's threat may be for nothing. But still... Beauregard mustn't find the locket. Truth Seekers couldn't lie without sacrificing their immortality, but she had to buy some time, at least until sunrise when Niniane would be weakened and her ghostly guards in their daytime hiding places. And Raphael, who had been nothing but kind to her and the ghosts on his ranch, didn't deserve to be tortured. She took a deep breath, the taste at the back of her mouth bitter with what she was about to do.

"It's not there." It pained Maggie to the core of her soul to tell the lie.

"Yes? Well?" Niniane leaned forward, her expression hungry.

Maggie wished she could enjoy her cousin's desperation, but she had to force out the words. "It's... Its buried deep in the ice at the South Pole."

"Oh." Niniane frowned. "At what coordinates?"

"The pole, what do you think?"

Niniane snapped her fingers. "I have an ice witch who owes me a favor."

PHILIPPE, who hadn't realized how attuned he'd become to Maggie, felt her lie to the core of his soul, and it broke his heart.

"No," he whispered.

"Your girl must be in dire circumstances, as we feared," Rothfeather told him. "Her kind can lie in emergencies, and..." He broke off.

"And what?"

"When they do..." He shook his head. "They lose their powers and become mortal like you."

Philippe leapt out of his chair. "But that means she's in even more danger now. They couldn't hurt her before." He looked around and spotted the door. "I've got to go for her."

A gnarled fist closed with an iron grip on his arm. "Now don't make me go poltergeist on ye, lad. Chances are they don't realize what she's done yet. She still has time."

"Until when?"

The hand eased up and pulled back into the shadows. "Until sunrise."

"Which is...?"

"In two hours."

"Will that give her enough time? Will it give me time to find her?"

"It depends on the lie she told and how quickly she's found out."

5

A raven's cawing woke Maggie. Strange... She'd not needed sleep before, not since she had been Margaret of Cornwall.

Then she remembered. She'd told a lie. She was a Truth Seeker no more. Ah, well, she had pondered retirement anyway. Maybe work at Raphael's ranch, something quiet, low-key. Maybe even settle down, have a family.

She shook her head. The thought had never crossed her mind before, but when she closed her eyes, she dreamed of a faceless man, his arms around her. But not Philippe—he was too innocent, his life only started. She needed to be with someone who would understand the lifestyle she'd led and the things she'd had to do.

But Philippe... She hoped the old pirate entertained him well. She knew she probably wouldn't even see the rest of her mortal life once Niniane found her out, but by then Roth-feather would have figured out what she was after and would send someone to safeguard it. He was a good sort, if a little gruff... A pirate who had taken the gentleman's way out.

Maggie squinted against the light that assaulted her blue

human eyes. What had they done with her glasses? With them on, she might still have a remnant of her power. She shifted and felt them in the pocket of her coat.

"Well well well..." Niniane held the torch close to Maggie's face. "Look who told a lie. I'll give it to you, Cousin—I didn't think you had it in you to give up your immortality like that."

Maggie looked through the flame and the smoke and saw Beauregard's sepulchral form. Her heart skipped a beat. Had he found it?

"It happens to all eventually," he intoned. "Unfortunately, I could not find it."

"That's all right, Beau." Niniane's voice was soft, sinister. "That means I get to have the pleasure of torturing it out of her."

Maggie exhaled. It was still safe...for now.

"I was saving that ice witch's favor, Margaret. You'll pay for having me waste it."

"How did you figure it out so quickly?"

"We have locations everywhere, dear sister, even at the South Pole. It's summer down there now, plenty of light, so all her snow beast had to do was look. But I digress... It will be fun to torture you. Your initiation to Avalon will seem like a pleasant memory after this."

PHILIPPE LOOKED DOWN at the ancient pistol in his hand.

"It has one bullet in it," Rothfeather cautioned him. "So make your shot good."

"Just one bullet?" Philippe had never handled a gun.

"It's silver with a cross engraved on it. It will stop her for a bit. That way you can rescue your girl. She must have a purpose in the plan if they've held her so long. You need to hurry. If The Lady can't get the truth out of her by daylight, she'll lose patience and kill her."

"The Lady?"

The old pirate nodded. "Niniane du Lac. Heard of her?"

Philippe recalled the name from English literature classes of long ago. "Of the King Arthur legend?"

"Let's just say she lasted a bit longer than he did, and she still causes trouble for mortals."

"Why is dawn the deadline?"

Rothfeather gestured to him. "You escaped. They know you'll come back for her, or that someone from her organization will find you and have you lead them to her. Niniane's guards won't be strong enough to stop you once the sun rises, and she doesn't like to be vulnerable."

A chill crawled up Philippe's neck. "How is shooting her going to stop her if she's immortal?"

"She's part faerie, so it won't kill her, but that which keeps her from dying also makes her vulnerable to certain charms, including silver bullets and the sign of the Christians. This bullet is doubly potent."

"What will it do?"

"She'll fall, bleed, and have to disappear for a day to—well, wherever she goes—to recuperate. It should buy you the time you need. Hurry now, lad, or your friend may be done for."

"Where are they?" Philippe stood and tucked the pistol into his belt.

"Thomas and Betsy will show you."

"You always had such a pretty face," Niniane told Maggie as she hit her the twentieth time. She'd started light with slaps, then progressed to punches and kicks, and now she held a silver knife, careful to only touch the hilt. Maggie, bruised and broken, sensed the sunrise and prayed that it would all be over with soon. If Niniane couldn't get the truth out of her by daylight, Maggie herself would be killed, but Maggie hoped her spirit would be strong enough to hang on long enough to let her fellow Truth Seekers know the location of the locket. It was a gamble. Maggie needed to get word to Philippe—if he'd come.

A certain lightening of the air indicated to Maggie that the time drew near. She closed her eyes and waited for the final blow.

PHILIPPE STOPPED in front of an old warehouse on the waterfront. Thomas, who had begun to fade as soon as they stepped outside in the pre-dawn light, put his translucent hand on the door.

"Aye, this is the place."

Philippe could feel it, too. The morning cold bit through his long woolen coat and heavy boots, and he hoped it would be warmer inside.

"Good luck, mate." With a final twist of his hand, Thomas unlocked the door, and Philippe crept inside.

At first, he heard nothing as his eyes adjusted to the darkness. It looked like Niniane's spirits, weakened by the sunlight, had all departed for their daily hiding places.

He felt along the wall and found a staircase. The odors of mold and rotten fish accosted his nose as he made his way down the metal stairs into the basement. Light flickered around a cracked wooden door and between the splintered wooden panels. A large black bird sat on a stool at the bottom of the stairs, and it blinked baleful red eyes at him. He crept to the door and looked in.

Maggie sat tied to a rotten wooden chair. A gorgeous blond woman with emerald eyes stood over her and held a knife, its tip bloodied by the long cut she had just carved down Maggie's bruised cheek. Blood dripped down the Truth Seeker's face and into her hair. Enraged, Philippe raised the pistol, but he told himself to wait for the right shot.

"Now that you're human again, you know what it's like to feel hate, don't you Margaret? I think that before you felt a little sorry for me."

"That was before you gave up your humanity entirely," Maggie whispered through clenched teeth.

"And you always liked to help humans. Or is it because you wanted to go back to being one yourself? Were you counting down the centuries until you could retire like Beauregard and live a normal life? Did you flirt with lying so you could escape the drudgery of eternal service? Did you ever know what it was like to love a mortal and want to be one so you could spend a lifetime together?"

Maggie didn't respond, and Philippe found himself wondering the same.

"It's daylight," Maggie whispered. With a movement too quick for human eyes, Niniane thrust the knife toward Maggie's abdomen. Philippe pulled the trigger, and Niniane flew back with the impact and disappeared.

"Maggie!" Philippe picked up the knife where it had fallen and cut Maggie loose. She held a hand over the bleeding wound, just beneath her rib cage. Philippe took off his coat and over-shirt and used the soft flannel to staunch the flow.

"Don't worry about me," Maggie gasped. "You have to find the locket. It's the one thing that can stop her."

"I have to get you to a hospital." His eyes welled with tears.

Maggie shook her head. "This is more important. You have to stop her."

"Where is it?"

"At Raphael's ranch. Find it today. Let the spirits guide you."

"How am I supposed to get there?" He didn't want to know the answer. "There's no time."

"The tunnels. Use them. You're the one mortal who can."

Her breath came in gasps, and Philippe carried her up the stairs. As he thought, they were in a deserted part of town. He staggered toward the sound of traffic and soon found a busy street.

"What happened to you there?" A policeman hailed them.

"She needs to get to a hospital," Philippe called. He pushed Maggie into the man's arms and sprinted away.

He ducked the raven that swooped over his head but lost sight of it between two buildings.

PHILIPPE FOUND the nearest chain coffee shop, crowded with the morning breakfast rush. His heart ached, but he figured that, of all the places to be stabbed, downtown Boston was a good one. He glanced over his shoulder every few seconds to see if he was being followed. He had blood on his hands, but he hadn't done anything wrong...except for hesitate those few crucial seconds.

The line inched forward. He'd looked, but there were no bathrooms, so he needed a plan to get to the store-room in the back through the "Employees Only" door. Philippe silently thanked Maggie for jumping them to Boston and not somewhere in the friendly, curious Southeast. No one made eye contact with him—he was just another worn-out, unshaven graveyard-shift worker in a long, black overcoat.

As he left the draught from the door, the warm air and smell of coffee enveloped him. He could feel the tunnel open, and his heart flipped. He would have to spill something, and, while the baristas cleaned it, slip back into the store-room.

He didn't have to wait long for the opportunity. An older man with a grizzled gray beard and wild black eyes bumped in to Philippe with his caramel mocha latte. A quick jostle, and the latte landed with a sticky splat on the floor. All motion stopped. Conversation ceased, and Philippe found himself the center of attention.

"Hey, buddy, what's your problem?" The old man glared at Philippe with bloodshot eyes.

"Whaddaya mean?" Philippe hoped that the drunk couldn't hear the fear in his voice. "You bumped into me."

The baristas looked more surly than perky as they wielded damp towels and hurried from behind the counter.

"That's okay, sir, Terry's making you another one." The barista shot Philippe an annoyed look as he bent down to swipe at the mess.

But Philippe wasn't there. When the crowd's attention shifted to the baristas, he ducked and slipped through the crowd to the back of the store. There he found a door that opened on to a long hallway. His nose told him in which direction the beans were stored—left, toward the enticing aroma, the pull of the tunnel more insistent.

Philippe paused. Was it withdrawal, or had he just never noticed how the tunnel called to him with his favorite mocha java aroma? Was it a trap? He heard the door creak behind him, and the hairs stood up on the back of his neck.

"What're ye waiting for lad, go through." The voice was Rothfeather's, but the feel wasn't.

"The right moment," Philippe said, his heart pounding.

"It's now, Philippe. Go!" Now it was Maggie who spoke an insistent whisper in his ear.

"I thought your kind couldn't be out during daylight James." Philippe turned to face Betsy's brother.

James lounged against the wall.

"The Lady taught me how." He spoke in his own voice now, a husky young tenor. Philippe could see from his barely-there transparency that he was weak. He may be able to appear after sunrise but it was unlikely that he could do anything. Or could he?

"May as well take directions from the devil," Philippe told him as he backed toward the room and frantically tried to make up his mind: was it a trap, or was it a ploy to buy time for someone to build one? He used his instincts, which urged him toward the tunnels, and he decided to trust them just as his hand found the knob.

He yanked the door open and lurched into the room. The bags took flight and whirled around him in a burlap cyclone.

"See if you can find it," James sneered.

Philippe reached up, and his fingertips brushed the magic bag. The moment's contact was enough, and with a thunderclap, he was thrown to his stomach and landed on a cold marble floor.

The smell of coffee assailed his nostrils in a thick, warm wave, and he gasped for air.

"Everyone has their own brand of hell, my little mouse," the voice close to his ear said, and a forked tongue caressed his earlobe in one long, rasping motion. "Welcome to yours."

Philippe tried to stand, but the floor tilted. They had him. The last thought through his mind before he passed out was that he had failed Maggie.

At least we'll be together soon.

6

Philippe opened his eyes, then squinted them against the blazing light. "Am I dead?" he found his tongue and asked. He was greeted by a low, sinister chuckle.

"Not quite, my young friend." A chill slid down Philippe's spine at the sound of Beauregard's voice. "That can be arranged, I'm sure, after you do one thing for me."

"What one thing is that?" Philippe tried to move his arms, but found them tied.

"I think you know. The Lady wants that locket."

"I don't know where it is." It wasn't entirely untrue – Maggie had told him it was at Raphael's ranch, but not where, and it was a big place.

"Perhaps I can jog your memory." Beauregard snapped his fingers, and the large halogen lamp switched off. As his eyes attempted to adjust to the gloom, Philippe used his other senses to determine where he was. The darkness was so complete that he must be somewhere underground, which was reinforced by the dank smell that assailed his nostrils. Not too far under, though, since the air was warm and humid. The leather straps that held him were slimy, and when he shuddered, he felt the grit of sand under his back.

"You humans are so slow," the voice rasped right next to his ear. Philippe strained away from it. "It's now dawn here, but I will return. And then you can make the choice of when you will die."

And Philippe was alone. Or so he thought.

"His power is limited, you know." A light flickered to his left, and he turned his head to see Raphael, who looked older and grayer but held a candle steady in one hand and leaned on a cane with the other. "But he will be a force to be reckoned with once he attains what the Lady has promised."

"How do you know?"

"How else would you corrupt a Truth Seeker?"

The old man hobbled over and, with trembling fingers, unbuckled the straps that held Philippe's arms and legs. The dim light revealed that he'd been strapped to a stone block in what looked like a torture chamber with axes, swords, and other weapons on hooks on the wall.

"This is an old wine cellar that we use during Halloween," Raphael explained. He gestured to the weapons. "All plastic, except the leather straps, as you felt."

Philippe nodded. He swung his feet over the side of the table.

"I am dying, Philippe." Raphael sat next to him on the waist-high stone slab. "And with me, the power of the ranch that keeps evil spirits at bay. That's how Beauregard was able to sneak in, but it weakened him."

"What do I do?" Blood returned to Philippe's extremities with prickling pain.

"Find the locket."

"Where? She didn't tell me anything specific, only to let the spirits be my guide."

Raphael shrugged. "You have until dusk to look."

· · ·

TRINA THE TRIAGE nurse was on duty when the cop brought the pale redhead dressed in black leather into the ER. She grabbed her tablet and approached him as he stepped back from the stretcher.

"Name?"

"None given."

"Was she robbed?" Trina clicked her tongue. A tourist, probably, and she looked like she'd been beaten up pretty good.

"No, she still has a wallet, but it's not hers."

"What's the name in the wallet, then?"

"It's a guy's, the same Joe who dumped her on me. Philippe Ormandie of Portland, Oregon."

Trina wrote "Ormandie" under last name, and the cop looked at her with a raised eyebrow.

"Well, it's better than Jane Doe. I think we already have one of those."

The cop laughed, and Trina could see he was her age, maybe younger.

"True that." They stopped at the door so Trina could get the rest of the info.

"So what happened?"

The cop opened his mouth to tell her, but what came out was, "I notice you're not wearing a wedding ring. How about I tell you over breakfast?"

Trina was taken aback for a moment, but when she began to refuse, she said instead, "Sure, I'd love to. I get off at eight."

The both stood there and blushed.

Why, Trina wondered, had her usual shyness been so overcome by the desire to tell the truth?

PHILIPPE FELT as though he had tapped every brick, turned every rug, and checked every bedpost, drawer, and cupboard in the place, and no luck. Raphael helped as much as he could, but the old man tired so easily that Philippe had sent him to bed after lunch. He entered the last area a few minutes before twilight.

Once again, Raphael appeared with a candle. "This is the wine, liquor, and coffee cellar," he explained as he let Philippe into a large store room. "I don't think she's ever been in here, but you can look."

Philippe's heart sank as he looked at what seemed to be a million dusty bottles of wine, and liquor, particularly tequila. One whole wall was stacked with coffee beans, at least twenty bags.

"What is it they say about truth and fine spirits?" Raphael's laugh was a wheeze. The old man patted Philippe on the shoulder and handed him the candle. In a daze, Philippe wandered down the rows and wondered where to begin. He felt he was in the right room, but every tick of his watch, which worked again, sounded his doom. He heard the tap of Raphael's cane on the stairs as he ascended for dinner.

Philippe held up the candle and peered into the bottles of mezcal, each with its own worm at the bottom of the glass cylinder. He felt sympathy for the poor creatures and hoped that their last moments had been spent in a blissful drunken stupor.

"Not a bad idea," he thought and reached for the nearest bottle. But his extra sense told him to put that one aside and grab the one behind it, which was caked with dust. He held it up to the candle in a toast, and when he did, something sparkled in the bottom. He looked closer and saw it wasn't a worm, but the locket. He shook his head. Maggie had told him to let the spirits be his guide—he just hadn't known which ones.

"Excellent job, Philippe." He spun around to see Beauregard, his raven on his shoulder, in the doorway.

Without thinking, Philippe unscrewed the bottle, upended

it, and took a huge swallow of mezcal. The locket on its chain scraped down the side of the bottle and into his throat. He didn't even feel it as the spirits set his mouth, esophagus, and stomach aflame.

With a howl, Beauregard leapt at him, his clawed fingers extended for Philippe's throat. Philippe ducked and swung the bottle at the ghoul. Beauregard dodged. He crashed into a shelf full of clay jugs, which shattered around him. The boozy smell of fermented cactus permeated the air, and Philippe made a dash for the door. Beauregard rose through the clay shards and loped after him.

Philippe ran, every step echoed by a thud of his heart and a flip of his stomach, through the long, dark, stone corridor. A cold draught passed through him—Beauregard. A wave of nausea and pain washed through Philippe, and he crashed to the ground. He rolled over, clutched his stomach and vomited. What had the ghost done to him? Or did magic locket not agree with him?

"That's it." Beauregard, now solid again, leaned over him. "Bring it back up."

Philippe found himself back in the Halloween dungeon. He looked around through tear-filled eyes for something to defend himself with. The plastic weapons appeared real enough, but it wasn't like they would work against a ghost. He swallowed hard and chewed the inside of his cheek to control the nausea. A metallic taste—blood?—coated his tongue.

"Look," he croaked, "I'm about finished. Why don't we just wait a while and see what happens?"

Beauregard's face looked even more skeletal in the gloom, but Philippe saw him raise an eyebrow. "What do you mean?"

He gestured to his abdomen and spat blood to clear his mouth. "It's going to come out one way or another."

"Time is of the essence, Philippe. The Lady doesn't like to

wait."

Maggie's pale face flashed through Philippe's mind, and he wondered if she'd gotten help in time. He took a deep breath and steeled himself for what he knew would be the consequences of his next statement.

"Then you'll never get it as long as I'm alive."

Beauregard smiled. "As I had hoped." He bared his fangs, and the odors of death, decay, and more blood washed over Philippe as the ghoul bent over him. Beauregard licked Philippe's neck in preparation for the fatal bite, and Philippe shuddered and reached into his special sense for whatever he might have left to fight the monster. He remembered how Maggie had summoned the ghoul in North Carolina, and he thought about her and what she stood for. Philippe remembered the look in her eyes, their golden wisdom so exquisite, and held the memory, the Truth Seeker's power. And her grief at what Beauregard had become.

A wave of betrayal and hurt washed over Philippe, and he fell hard to the floor as Beauregard dropped him, clawed hands over his eyes. Philippe turned and vomited blood.

Beauregard staggered backward and clung to the doorframe. "Very well, Philippe. Margaret did give you a charm to protect yourself. Or maybe you already had it, a love for truth. But Raphael is dying, and no one will come to this room until Halloween, which is, what? Nine months from now."

Philippe's heart sank to his stomach. He needed to be in a hospital, not a dungeon where no one would find him for months.

"Fare thee well, or rather, poorly." Beauregard grinned at his own pun. "I shall retrieve the locket from your corpse." The monster slammed the door and Philippe heard him drag something heavy to block it. Not that he could have handled the iron-studded wooden door itself in his current state... He stretched out on the gritty, cold floor and closed his eyes.

As consciousness faded, he remembered Maggie's golden gaze.

MAGGIE LEANED against the wall of the operating room in spirit form and watched the surgeons working on her body. They'd bandaged her cheek to stop it from bleeding and focused on the stab wound. She'd been injured before in her line of work, but not since she'd been granted the near-immortality of being a Truth Seeker.

"That's going to hurt like hell when you wake up."

Maggie turned to see a generally nondescript man of medium build, wavy brown hair, and golden eyes. If she'd had a body, she would have sighed with resignation.

"Merlin. Why am I not surprised to see you here?"

"Well, I am your supervisor." He shook his head, and even after all these centuries, his disappointment stung. "What in the world did you get yourself into?"

"A trap. Niniane wanted her locket back." She slid a sideways glance at Merlin. He still held a grudge against the Lady for locking him in a tree trunk for a thousand years. Blinded by love, he'd not seen the trap coming until it was too late. Then he'd gone willingly, in denial to the end that her frustration and bitterness over the end of Avalon had turned her against them all.

To his credit, he only shrugged. "It figures. She was never one to give up easily. But how did she manage to trick *you*?"

"One of my contacts betrayed me. Beauregard."

"That old ghost?" He shook his head. "Should've guessed he'd be one to turn bad."

She didn't know if he spoke to himself or her. Either way, she should have figured out something was amiss, and Merlin, ever the teacher, wouldn't let her off the hook so easily.

He didn't. "And...?" he prompted.

"And I got careless. I got caught up in the glamor of zapping myself and our target around to different places, showing off what I could do." She rubbed her eyes even though she had no physical sensations. "I never could resist a good rescue."

He put a hand on her ghostly shoulder. "That's both a strength and a weakness. We have the chance to gain and use something powerful—Niniane's locket."

"Right. We technically already have it."

"It's in a safe place...for now," he agreed. "But not where you left it. We need someone to retrieve it, and you're still the best person for the job."

If her spirit form had a heart, it would have sped up with hope. "Does that mean I'm still a Truth Seeker in spite of the lie?"

"Yes, provided you can get the locket. The young man trusts you, so it makes sense for you to get it from him. Besides," he added and shifted his weight. "I've been arguing against the 'no lying' rule for a while. It's just not practical anymore."

"Oh, thank you!" She threw her arms around Merlin and hugged him. Even in spirit form, he still smelled vaguely of damp earth and wet wood.

"Right, ahem." He stepped back. "Oh, and something else to keep in mind. We're short-staffed, so I've recruited a few humans to help us out in local jurisdictions. It's an experiment."

"Okay." She didn't know how that would work, but Merlin didn't do anything without thorough research.

"Once they wheel you into recovery, you should be able to zap yourself out of here. And your cheek will heal, but there will be a faint scar since she used a ceremonial dagger."

"Of course she did." Maggie rubbed her hands together, impatient for the doctors to finish. She'd get out of there, find Philippe, get the locket back, and regain her good favor with her bosses. How hard could it be?

. . .

PHILIPPE FLOATED through clouds of gloom and nightmare flashes of fear, searching for something to bring him to consciousness. All the while, he held the vision of Maggie's eyes in front of him, their golden light a beacon of hope. When a warm hand clasped his, he opened his eyes, and the vision resolved into reality—a hospital room—and he wasn't alone.

"Welcome back, stranger," Maggie said. She looked a little more pale and thin, and there was a faint scar across her left cheek, but she was there. Alive.

"You're okay?" he asked. And then he saw her eyes. "You've got your job back?"

She smiled, the expression in her eyes a mix of happiness and exhaustion. "I'm okay as much as I can be. And yes. My superiors reviewed the situation and decided that my lie was warranted."

A pang of disappointment speared him. "So you're still a Truth Seeker?"

She nodded. "And you're my next assignment."

Philippe's heart skipped a beat. That sounded promising. "Oh?"

"Yes, I need the locket." She leaned over him. "Do you have it on you?"

"Not exactly." He pointed to his stomach. "I have it in me. I swallowed it."

"Oh." She rubbed her temples. "This is going to be harder than I thought."

"Why?" Now his stomach fluttered like it knew they discussed its contents. "Can't we just wait for it to, um, appear?"

She shook her head. "It won't. Its magic is such that it will slowly poison you from the inside until you die, and then Niniane can retrieve it from your corpse."

Philippe clutched his stomach. Was that an extra prick of pain? "How long will it take?"

"A few days, maybe a week." Then she echoed Beauregard's words, which filled Philippe with terror. "Niniane doesn't like to wait."

"Okay, what do we do?" He struggled to sit, and she helped him. He didn't know if it was the ordeal with Beauregard or the locket, but he felt weak. And helpless. How was he going to do anything in this state?

"We go to a friend of mine who may be able to help. She's in Atlanta."

"And we're...?" The hospital room gave him no clues as to his location.

"In San Antonio. I don't dare try to zap us with the locket inside you, so we'll have to take the slow way—airplane."

"I trust you." He grabbed her hand. "It will be romantic, traveling the old-fashioned way with just the two of us."

She pulled her hand from his. "We can't be romantic."

"Why not?" He spread his hands. "I'm a dying man."

"Professional boundaries. And..."

"And what?"

She had a point, but... Had she tricked him? Or had he hoped for more than was actually there? She hesitated, her bottom lip between her teeth.

"What is it?" he asked. "After all we've been through, you know you can trust me."

"You're right. You didn't have to risk your life to come back for me. Or go look for the locket." She took a deep breath. "I'm cursed."

Okay, that wasn't what he expected. "What do you mean?"

"When I asked the Oracle about my terrible luck in love, she said, *If you are to love or to be loved, to share possession of heart and soul, then woe to he to whom this gift is given, for he will be destroyed.*"

"The Oracle?" Philippe remembered something from Greek

mythology. "Wait, the King Arthur legend people were affected by Greek mythology? That's some crazy mashup."

"All our legends are connected." She made a broad gesture. "And they still live on, just not always in this dimension."

Philippe didn't want to talk about multiple dimensions. He had more pressing problems. "Can you do anything about the curse? Can your friend?"

"No." Her tone told him further questioning would be futile, that she'd given up.

"Fine." He acknowledged his pouting. "It will have to do for now." But was he already cursed? He definitely had started to feel something for her. How could he not? She'd risked her own immortality—and his mind tripped over that concept—to keep the human race safe. And in a moment of vulnerability, she'd cried in his arms after Beauregard's betrayal. He wanted to get to know her—Maggie the woman, not Maggie the Truth Seeker —better. Was that enough to doom him?

Well, uncertainty made life interesting. And he suspected his life had just reached heights of interesting he had no idea existed. First they'd get the locket removed, then he'd help her tackle her curse.

PART II

THE LOCKET

7

B y the time they got everything straightened out with the hospital, who let Philippe go against medical advice, the sky had turned almost completely dark. Philippe barely paid attention to his surroundings as the cab whisked them through turn after uncomfortable turn. When they finally arrived at the terminal, Maggie had him wait on a bench while she went to stand in the line for tickets. He agreed to join her when he needed to show his ID to the ticket agent. He half-monitored her progress in line and half-attended to the other people around them. He could prove he was useful, if not capable of much at the moment, by looking for trouble.

One man in particular caught his attention. Something felt off about the guy, although he looked harmless enough in a sharp gray suit with a black upscale my-luggage-is-more-important-than-your-luggage carry-on. Maybe that was it—he stood out among the more casual traveling crowd. And kept looking at Philippe.

Philippe glanced away, not wanting to seem like he was star-ing. But it didn't surprise him when the man approached. He only hoped it was a case of mutual curiosity and nothing more sinister, although something like an electric charge raced along his skin when the man sat beside him.

"Traveling will wear you out," the man said. He leaned forward, his elbows on his knees.

Philippe nodded, but didn't make eye contact. Instead he checked on Maggie's position. She only had a couple of people in front of her.

"Is that your girlfriend? The redhead?"

Philippe shrugged. "Not exactly. We're just friends." He almost laughed at the absurdity. Friends that fate had shoved together thanks to a stupid locket that currently spewed poison in his stomach.

"But you want something more."

It wasn't a question, so Philippe didn't respond. Not that it was the guy's business, anyway. But he persisted, and the more he spoke, the more Philippe caught some sort of accent— Eastern European, maybe?

"A pretty girl like that, I wouldn't let her get away."

"Look," Philippe turned toward him to tell him to shut up, but his phone dinged. Maggie was texting him that it was their turn. He stood. "It's none of your damn business what our relationship is."

The man only shrugged, his palms up. "And the fact you are getting so upset means I'm right. Remember—some things are worth fighting for. She's a special woman. I can tell."

"You have no idea," Philippe muttered and went to join Maggie at the ticket counter.

"No, we don't have any bags," she was saying. "It's a quick trip, only for the night. We've heard it's a great place to party."

Philippe handed over his ID and tried to smile and look like he felt up for partying. A dull ache in the pit of his stomach reminded him that it was the last thing he wanted to do. But he'd play along if it would help solve his problem.

He watched Maggie charm the gate agent, her eyes hidden

by purple lenses again, and for a moment, he felt better. Maybe the strange guy was right. Maybe she was worth fighting for, even if she didn't think so.

MAGGIE AND PHILIPPE made it through security with no hassle, and the flight ran on time. She thought she'd seen him talking to someone, but he shrugged off her questions. Maggie hadn't been through many airports since her abilities allowed her to zap herself to wherever she needed to be, but occasionally her work demanded it. The press of people with all their emotions —a lot of frustration—made her feel claustrophobic, so she conserved her energy and didn't press him. Soon enough they were seated on the plane, and he fell asleep. Not that she blamed him. It had been a grueling day for him in more ways than one.

She took the opportunity to examine him more closely as the plane took off. His dark stubble stood out against his washed-out skin, and purple shadows ringed his eyes—the locket's dark work. And the aftermath of his encounter with Beauregard, which may have cracked his soul. She hadn't told him that. He had enough to worry about. She'd heard Truth Seekers who'd turned could use their powers to disrupt the spiritual energy in another being, like they had when seeking information, but in a darker way. That would mend eventually, but what was Niniane's locket doing to him? She hoped Lucia would have an answer. Maggie couldn't shake the fear that removing it wouldn't be as simple as a surgery. Evil objects had their own defenses.

What had possessed him to swallow it? It had been a snap judgment with grave consequences, but she'd sensed the potential for impulsive actions in him. That sort of spontaneity would likely make him attractive to other women, especially considering his dark good looks, but while she could admire a quick mind and handsome face, she'd never liked bad boy behavior. She wished she could talk to Raphael about his impressions of Philippe, but of course she couldn't call him from the plane. And Raphael had enough of his own problems. Plus, while he had some comprehension of supernatural affairs, he wasn't in law enforcement.

She gazed into the night, at the disappearing city lights that slid below the shadow of the plane's wing, and wished she could talk to someone who would understand what it was like to always be hunting or hunted. Or both, like she was now.

She turned her thoughts to planning, which always soothed her soul when troubled.

The flight passed quickly, and they touched down early. Philippe woke with a start.

"What? Where am I?"

She touched his shoulder to soothe him. "Atlanta. You slept the whole time." When he relaxed, she removed her hand.

"Oh." He looked disappointed. "Are you okay?"

She refrained from telling him that she could defend herself better than he could imagine. Well, in spite of how it might seem after the disaster in Boston. Instead, she only nodded. "Good nap?"

"Yes." He looked away.

"Did you dream?" It would be just her luck if her enemies were trying to get to him through the Collective Unconscious.

"Nope. At least not that I can remember." He rubbed his eyes. "Are we going to get food soon?" His stomach echoed the question with a growl.

She couldn't help a grin at his very human question. She had to remind herself again of his mortal needs. "Appetite is a good sign. And yes, once my colleague drops us off at my condo, I'll go get us something."

"Good." He leaned back and didn't say anything until they'd deplaned and walked through the airport, just two more faces in a sea of them. The sensations of everyone being too close, too ready to bump into them with their messy feelings, had disappeared once they'd reached the controlled environment of the plane. But now the emotional claustrophobia returned, and she didn't feel like she took a full breath until they stood outside at the arrivals area. She looked for Lucia's white Saturn. It was an unusual color for a no-longer-produced car—like a ghost, but it fit.

Finally she spotted it and waved, and Lucia pulled up. Lucia unfolded her six-foot-plus frame from the driver's seat and shook out her braids, which this week hung thick and dark around her face.

"Margaret," she said, her Caribbean accent rolling the syllables off her tongue. "It's good to see you."

"Thank you for picking us up." Maggie hugged her. Although the woman had a lot of physical and supernatural power, she gave gentle squeezes. Maggie had always admired her restraint. "This is Philippe."

"Nice to meet you." Philippe held out a hand, then pulled it back halfway when he almost toppled over. Poor boy. She really needed to get him some food. If she hadn't been so overwhelmed, she would have suggested they grab a snack in the airport.

Oh, well, they'd be at their destination, which was surrounded by restaurants, soon enough.

"Ah." Lucia shook his hand, and Maggie sensed the magical probe Lucia sent into Philippe's body. Only a twitch of Lucia's eyebrows indicated she'd sensed something amiss. "Come, you must be exhausted."

"And hungry." He got into the backseat, where he slumped, his arms crossed.

"So you are on assignment?" Lucia asked once they'd pulled into traffic.

"Yes. The coffee shop tunnels."

"Ah. I have heard about them. And that they were using the pathways to open doors between the shops."

The intermittent glare from the streetlights overhead and vehicles on the other side of the interstate stung Maggie's eyes, and she rubbed them. "That's not good news. That means they could attack us from anywhere."

"You will have to be extra careful. But I sense you have an ally you are not yet aware of."

Philippe straightened. "Wait, who's going to attack? And how does she know this stuff?"

Maggie glanced back at him. "Lucia's a psychic. The real deal. And we'll have to watch for Niniane and her creatures. Hopefully she hasn't caught on as to where we are yet, but it's only a matter of time before she follows the locket."

"Great." Philippe slumped back again and looked out of the window.

Maggie caught Lucia up on what had happened with Philippe filling in what she didn't yet know.

"So you swallowed the locket to keep it away from Beauregard?" Lucia asked with a chuckle. "He must have been furious."

"Yes." Philippe grinned. "He was pissed."

Okay, so maybe it hadn't been such a dumb move, only a desperate one. But it had left Maggie with a major problem.

Lucia dropped them off in front of a condo complex in Decatur. Maggie found the key and the code in her pocket and let them in. She supported Philippe, who seemed to have grown yet weaker. Or...

"Are you okay?" she asked. "Do I need to take you to the hospital?"

"No." He eased back. "I'm okay."

"You were just leaning on me because you could." She glanced at him sideways while she unlocked the door.

"Guilty." He shrugged. "You can't blame a guy for trying."

Had he not heard her when she'd said he should stop

trying? She bit her tongue before she blew up at him. Although she didn't need sleep, she did want a nice hot bath and to relax, but she also needed to get away from him, especially if he was getting clingy. "Go make yourself comfortable. I'll be back with food."

"Is it safe?" He peered into the darkness. She reached past him and flipped on the lights, which revealed a living room with cream-colored carpet and blue couches in an L-shape facing a television. The blinds were closed over what would be a nice set of windows during the daytime.

"Yes, it's warded, which means that no supernatural creature can enter uninvited."

"Right. Good." He staggered to the couch and flopped on it. "I'll be right here when you get back."

Of course now he'd made her anxious, so she checked the place. Nothing hid in either of the bedrooms or bathrooms, or in any of the closets.

"Don't open the door for anyone," she warned him. "And try to remain alert if you can. You have my phone number should you need me. I'll just be down the street picking up pho. Is that okay?"

"Pho sounds perfect." He smiled at her. "Thanks for taking care of me."

"You're welcome." For some reason, his words annoyed her. She let herself out and locked the door behind her.

8

Maggie tucked her hair under her hat. She walked out of the back entrance of the condo complex in case Niniane had found them and had someone watching the front door. She paused, opening her senses to the surroundings. To her right, parking decks on either side of the drive would make perfect hiding places for dastardly creatures. A small garden to her left could also conceal something or someone. The air held a slight whiff of sulfur toward the garden, so she turned the other direction. When she'd passed midway along the parking decks, one of the shadows detached itself from the wall and darted to stand in front of her before she could evade it.

"You have something we want," it said. Its pale face and extended fangs said vampire, a hungry one at that judging from the red glow around its irises.

Maggie backed up and reached in her pocket for her pistol, which was loaded with silver-tipped bullets. Vampires loved her scent. Something about her being human with immortal essence drove them crazy.

A voice from behind her made her shudder. "I wouldn't do that if I were you."

She bumped into another one, and it wrenched her hat off with one hand while grabbing her by the hair with the other. She simultaneously slammed one elbow into its solar plexus and kicked backwards with the other foot. Its kneecap crunched under her heel, and it let go with a howl.

But that had given the other one the chance to attack, and it tackled her. She tried to crawl away, but it grabbed her by her feet and clawed its way up her legs. It paused to run a tongue along one gash on her leg. The whoosh of something flying through the air made her cover her head, and the vampire stiffened, then dissolved into smoke and ash. A small stake clattered to the ground.

A change in air pressure above her warned her the one she'd injured had recovered and was attacking again. She grabbed the stake, then jammed it into its throat. It, too, vanished. But the sulfur smell remained. She scrambled to her feet and then rolled as something foul-smelling flew over her. She pulled out her pistol and got a shot off, but it missed and cracked against the brick of the parking deck. She wedged herself into a space where she had a brick wall at her back, but she remained exposed from all other directions.

Don't be stupid. There could be humans around. But she doubted it. Something about were-bats drove them off. Not just the smell, but their sense of *wrongness*.

So Niniane had stationed vampires on one side and were-bats on the other. Maggie smiled. That meant her cousin was worried. Which meant that Maggie could somehow use the power of the locket to defeat her even with it being inside of Philippe.

And with a stab of sadness, Maggie had to let go of the denial that Niniane could be saved. If she had partnered with the dark creatures, little hope remained.

The were-bat came for another pass, and Maggie got a clear shot. It tumbled backwards, but just as the vamps had used the one to distract her from the other, another were-bat jumped down from above. She darted out of her hiding place, and something else shot the second were-bat. It landed on the ground with a thud.

Maggie rose to her feet, gun in hand, reminding herself to breathe and be aware of whatever else may be out there. Or whoever else. Was the mysterious shooter the ally Lucia had mentioned?

"You can show yourself," she called. "I think that was it."

A black-helmeted figure leaned over the second floor of the parking deck, and Maggie covered her mouth so she wouldn't gasp. Had she fought one set of dark creatures to be faced by yet another, more sinister one? In the two seconds it took for the strange being to remove its helmet, she ticked though all the possibilities of what it could be—troll, dark fae, dark elf, high imp—and what she'd need to do to defend herself.

She exhaled with relief when the helmet revealed not an it, but a he. A very handsome he with bright blue eyes, blond hair damp and curly from being under the helmet, and a square jaw. The best part—his full lips held a grin that said he'd enjoyed the fight as much as she had.

"Down in a second," he said.

Maggie took the few seconds to compose herself. Who was this dark knight? Wait, not a knight, although he did remind her of the ones she'd known in her very distant past. The legends hadn't quite managed to portray how fun they were, and she'd almost forgotten herself. But when she saw him again, she wondered if he perhaps held the soul of one of her old friends reincarnated.

Don't be a fool. You can't get hopeful now—you're still cursed for what you did.

"Charles Allen MacKenzie at your service," he said and bowed over the hand she'd held out to shake.

Oh, gods. The increased tempo of her heart, which she hadn't been aware of in ages, warned her she needed to get away from him fast.

"Uh, Margaret Livingstone," she said, using the first surname she'd come up with after being made a Truth Seeker.

He straightened. She tried not to, but she couldn't help but notice how well he wore the modern body armor, his helmet under his arm, and a small crossbow in a holster at his waist.

Then she recognized her rudeness, inexcusable even outside of the age of chivalry. "Thank you for your help with the vamps and were-bats. I was caught unprepared."

Rather than gloat and preen like many men of her acquaintance would, he replied, "And thank you for your help. There were more than I could have handled on my own. I should've brought my team." He shrugged. "My intel was faulty, but that's no excuse."

Maggie closed her mouth. Humble and handsome and charming. Yep, time to go. But she needed to know more in case this was the ally Lucia had meant.

"Who's your team?"

He cocked his head. "Why don't you tell me who you really are, Margaret Livingstone... Of Cornwall?"

Heat flooded her face, and she took a step back. "Why don't you tell me how you know who I really am?"

A car entered the alley, and they moved to the sidewalk.

"Let's talk somewhere private," he suggested.

She could think of lots of things she would like to do with him in private—*bad Margaret, bad!*—which meant she really needed to get away from him.

"I'm on an important errand. Why don't I call you later?" She walked toward the street.

He stopped by a police car parked just before the alley met

the road and dropped his helmet and Kevlar vest in the front seat, leaving him in black pants and turtleneck. After securing the car and running his fingers through his hair to make it less flat, he moved to join her.

"Your phone number?" she asked, holding her phone. Now she burned with curiosity. He was a cop? What kind of place was Decatur?

"You just got ambushed by two vamps and two were-bats. I'd be a terrible cop if I didn't accompany you."

"You're a policeman?"

"Yes, a Lieutenant. Special detective, actually. Well, here they call us investigators. I'll give you the whole story when we talk on our own."

She tore her gaze away from his lips. His smile reminded her of someone, but she couldn't figure out who. "Suit yourself. I'm not going far."

They chatted like two regular people as she walked to the Asian fusion place around the corner.

"How long have you been in town?"

"Just got in."

Then, when she picked up two orders, he asked, "Who did you travel with?"

"Don't you know?" she teased as they walked out.

"I only heard about *you*." His tone had dropped an octave, and she shivered, but in a good way.

"I have a human with me. He's injured, and he needs food." She didn't want to say everything, of course.

"Understood." He didn't seem jealous or curious. She ignored the swirl of disappointment in her gut. "Let me have your number, and I'll give you mine, and we can chat later. I've got a secure app—both in terms of modern and less than modern spies—I use with my team. I'll text you the link."

"Okay." Secure apps? Mini-stake-throwing crossbows? She'd been making do with whatever technology she could find or cobble together, so she hoped she could at least get some of that information from him.

They exchanged numbers, and he walked her to the condo entrance.

"Good night, Margaret."

Damn, those lips. She focused on his bright blue eyes. That wasn't much better for keeping her heart rate down.

"Good night, Lieutenant MacKenzie."

"You can call me Charlie."

She almost replied with, "And you can call me anytime." But stuck with, "And I'm Maggie. But never Mags."

"Understood." He stepped back into the shadows and watched her key in her code.

She resisted the impulse to turn and wave once she was inside. Her steps echoed the mantra in her thoughts—*idiot, idiot, idiot.*

When she reached her door and opened it, she walked in to find Philippe standing behind the table and lighting a candle. He'd apparently done some exploring and found a red table-cloth, candles, and nice dishware. And flowers had appeared from somewhere—she thought they might have been in one of the bedrooms, but she hadn't paid that much attention.

"Oh, good, you're back." He gestured to the table. "What do you think?"

"I..." She took another look at the romantic setup. "I don't know what to think."

Without another word, she set the bags down on the kitchen counter, walked into the largest bedroom, and closed the door before he could see the tears of frustration and grief that she'd always be alone.

"WAS IT SOMETHING I SAID?" Philippe stood outside of Maggie's door. He thought he heard her crying, but he wasn't sure. What had he done wrong? He'd only tried to set a nice table. Okay, it did look romantic. *Was* romantic. But was it wrong to keep trying?

Finally she opened the door, and he stepped back when he saw her red, puffy eyes. Yep, she'd been crying. He moved to hug her, but she stopped him with a palm against his chest.

"No. I've told you. We have to keep this professional." The tears had made her voice husky, and it only drew him in more.

"Can I at least ask what's wrong?"

She squeezed past him and gestured to the table. "A candle-light dinner? Are you trying to get yourself killed? Remember the curse."

"I'm dying anyway with the locket in my stomach." He shrugged. "Why don't we just make the most of the time I have left?"

She looked back at him over her shoulder, and the coldness in her gaze punched him in the solar plexus. "Because I'm not interested in you that way."

"Is there someone else?" He hadn't mentioned it, but he'd been looking out of the window and had seen her walking across the street with a blond guy dressed in all black.

"No. There can't be." She flicked the lights on.

"Oh." He didn't believe her, but he walked to the table and blew out the candles. "Well, I guess we should just eat, then. Like two normal human beings. It will have to do for now."

"Except I'm not normal," she muttered and took the food out of the bag. They each fixed their pho and sat at the table. Maggie seemed lost in thought, but Philippe's disappointment wouldn't let him be silent. If she was going to keep putting him off, he needed all this to be over and to go home.

"When is Lucia going to come back and examine me? Wasn't that the plan?" He couldn't imagine what a magical examination would be like, but he didn't think it would be pleasant.

"She already did. She's likely back at her place researching to see what can be done. She'll call when she finds something."

"Oh." He was never going to figure all this stuff out. "I just want to go home."

She finally looked up from her food and gave him a soft expression. Sure, her face showed pity rather than love or attraction, but he'd take it. "I'm sure you do. This has been a lot."

He nodded, his throat tight. "This can be fixed, right? I can be healed and go back to normal."

"I hope so." She returned her attention to her bowl. "But some things can't be fixed."

He sensed she no longer spoke about his situation, but he didn't feel like asking questions he wouldn't get answers to. They finished up in silence, and she sent him to bed while she cleaned up.

"You need to conserve your strength. It may not feel like it but the locket is poisoning you inside."

"So you've said." He tried not to sound irritable, but he didn't want the reminder.

"Philippe, please." She walked over to him and put a hand on his arm. "The poison isn't just physical, but emotional. Please be careful. Try to guard your dreams if you can."

He nodded but didn't say anything. If she wasn't going to tell him what he needed to know—like the identity of that blond man she was walking with—then he didn't want to bother with her advice. He jerked away and walked into the second bedroom. The last sound he heard before he closed the door was her sigh.

Fine. Let her be frustrated for once.

Someone had stocked the bedroom and bathroom with pajamas, clothes, and toiletries for a guy. He cleaned up—the shower felt so good after the hospital and airplane—and put on the pajamas. They fit him perfectly, but an itchy wave of annoyance washed over him, starting from his stomach. How dare they—whoever they were—tell him where to go, what to do, even what to think and wear? He turned down the bed and flopped into it. Okay, that didn't suck. He'd get a good night's sleep and figure out what to do in the morning.

The man in the airport had been wrong—some things weren't worth fighting for. He wrapped the cozy flannel sheets and comforter around him and fell fast asleep before his brain could have another thought.

Philippe found himself back in the coffee shop in the San Antonio airport. The red tile outside the glass windows seemed duller, and the scene lacked the sunlight of when he'd last been there. When he tried to walk out of the shop, something invisible blocked him.

A shot of adrenaline made his heart gallop into his throat—had they finally caught him? Would Niniane appear and rip her locket from his stomach?

A noise behind him made him turn, and he saw the man in the gray suit he'd spoken with earlier.

"I'm sorry, did I startle you?" The gentleman smiled but didn't show his teeth.

"Yes." Philippe turned, his fists clenched. "Who are you? I'm tired of these games." Maggie had said to guard his dreams, but he didn't know what to do.

The man held out his hands palms-down in a placating gesture. "I only want to help. You've gotten yourself in quite a pickle, I see."

It was hard to fear a man who used phrases like "gotten yourself in a pickle," but Philippe remained wary. "Yes, I'm dealing with some stuff."

"More than just some stuff." The man sat at one of the small tables and gestured for Philippe to join him.

Philippe sat but remained half-turned. Not that he could get far, but at least he could jump out of the way if he needed to. "Okay, a lot of stuff."

"But having a good woman by your side can make it all worth it." He snapped his fingers, and an image of Maggie appeared beside the table. She smiled like he'd just told a funny joke, and Philippe wanted to hear her laugh.

"She's not for me." Philippe turned his head so he'd only see her from his peripheral vision. "She said she's not interested."

"She's a strong, determined woman." Her image disappeared with another snap of his fingers. "I've known her for quite a while. She's convinced herself that she is not worthy of love."

"What?" Philippe couldn't imagine that. "How? She's strong, brave, smart...beautiful."

"But she has a past, as we all do." The man drummed his fingers on the table, and the light sparked off a large ruby in an intricately carved ring on his left ring finger. Although clear, the stone looked like crystallized blood.

"What kind of past?" Philippe leaned forward.

"Has she told you who she is, really?"

"No." Now Philippe's frustration with her returned. "She's good at dodging the question."

"She is Margaret of Cornwall, the aunt of King Arthur who was lost to historical record once she joined the Truth Seekers, an interdimensional organization that fancies itself our law enforcement."

"Inter-what?" His mind tripped over what the man had just said. He'd accepted she was a cop, but the lost aunt of King Arthur? "That's not possible. I remember those stories. There was no Margaret of Cornwall, and even if there was, she'd be fifteen hundred years old by now."

"She has been allowed to not age, although she could retire and continue a normal human life span, find a lover, have children... But she believes herself to be cursed."

"She's said that."

The man stabbed a finger into the wood of the table. "But

curses are as much in a person's mind as they are in their body and soul. She could break it if she so desired to put forth the effort to find out how. But her biggest obstacle is herself."

The warmth of hope blossomed in Philippe's chest. "So if she figured out how to break the curse, I may have a chance with her."

"Right. She's not open to love from anyone as long as she believes she can't break the curse." He folded his hands. "I believe you are the one who can change her mind."

Philippe recalled her reaction to his attempt at a romantic dinner. He shook his head, but the seed of hope the man's words planted wouldn't quit. "But I don't even know if I've got the rest of a human life to live." He gestured to his stomach. "I've got to get rid of this thing."

"I will assist you when the time comes. First allow Margaret to set up her ritual. You'll know what to do from there."

"Wait, what ritual?"

But the dream faded, and Philippe found himself back in the bed in the condo. Maggie's voice came through the door, but he couldn't make out the words. Now wide awake, he decided to apologize for being an ass.

9

M aggie cleaned up the dinner dishes after Philippe went to bed. The repetitive domestic motions soothed her. Whereas she'd heard most people hated doing chores, mundane household tasks provided oases of normalcy in her otherwise strange existence. Granted, today had been unusually odd, but she hadn't ever lived what could be called a normal life. Not that she'd ever wanted to. From the time she was little, she'd played more with the boys and eschewed traditional "girl" things, as much as she was allowed. She'd left feminine activities to her older sisters, Morgause and Igraine, and her parents had indulged her, the youngest child.

She scrubbed the dishes harder when the memories of what had come next popped into her head—priestess training on Avalon under Niniane. Her studies had given her discipline, but she'd never lost her sense of adventure. And that's what had gotten her in trouble and why she still had to atone.

A chirp from her cell phone brought her back into the present, and she took a deep breath. She'd long since figured out that beating herself up wasn't useful, but her thoughts slid down that hole when she wasn't careful.

The text told her Lucia had arrived and waited to be buzzed in. She did so, but now her dark thoughts turned to the present. If Lucia needed to give her the news in person, it couldn't be good. She wondered if she could get the charming Lieutenant Charles Allen MacKenzie to share access to his secure communication system so she and Lucia could use it.

"What are you smiling about?" Lucia asked when Maggie opened the door. "It's not an expression I see on you often."

Maggie sighed. "Oh, the usual. A nice guy I can't pursue anything with."

Lucia inclined her head toward the second bedroom, her brows lifted in a question.

"No, someone else I met today." The image of Charlie's lips came to mind. "He reminds me of someone. Of course, I've lived so long that most people remind me of someone I've met in the past, but this feels significant."

"Ah. I'm sure you'll figure it out." Thankfully she didn't persist. Lucia knew about the curse but hadn't been able to give Maggie any help or direction with it. "I have done some reading and a divination ritual about the young man's problem."

"Tea?" Maggie always preferred bad news to be delivered with or immediately prior to a hot beverage. She was English, after all.

"Yes, please. Orange spice if you have it. It's too late for me to drink caffeine."

Maggie filled the electric kettle—one of her favorite modern inventions—and turned it on. "I'm pretty sure they stocked us up with a variety. Ah, here we are." She found the wooden box with the tea bags and pulled out one for Lucia and a strong English Breakfast for herself. She found the mugs easily.

Lucia stood on the other side of the counter between the kitchen and living room. "One thing I must warn you of is that the young man is being poisoned."

"We're already aware of that. Niniane's locket is powerful, and I have evidence that she's allied herself with the dark creatures. She wouldn't be able to if she hadn't turned to evil." The thought of her former mentor's damnation still made Maggie's heart hurt. "Do you think she may be cursed?"

"I don't know. But I'm not sure that's the source of the young man's poisoning. Just please be careful."

"I always am. Well, mostly. If I've learned anything over the past few days, it's that I need to be more so. I'll talk to him." She poured boiling water into the mugs over the waiting bags. As always, the smells of steam and tea leaves soothed her, no matter how much she'd been through.

Lucia accepted her mug. "My instinct is that you do not speak with him too much of our plans."

Maggie looked up from the darkening water in her mug with a frown. "I've already kept so much from him, and I do need him to trust us."

"Then tell him all that is necessary, but no more." She pulled the bag from her mug and threw the soggy paper sachet into the trash.

Maggie did the same, and they sat on the couches. Maggie wrapped her hands around her mug. It seemed that lying, or at least telling partial truths, would be part of the job, after all. "All right, what did you figure out? From what I can tell, our options are surgery or ritual. Or both."

"When I shook his hand, I felt the dark energy to his fingertips." Lucia gave a delicate shudder. "We do not have much time before it eats through him completely."

"Is emergency surgery warranted?" Maggie had heard of an ER doctor at the nearby Dekalb Medical Center who wasn't quite human.

"Even if we were to surgically remove the locket, we would need to clear the energy or it will still kill him."

Maggie mentally sifted through ritual options. "Hmmm,

and what do you think about surgery first so we wouldn't be fighting the locket's energy renewing itself?"

"Once an object like that joins with a human, it has protections. Breaching the human's skin will cause a fatal reaction."

"Damn, I was afraid something like that may be the case. And there are likely protections we don't know about yet. So, ritual it is."

"Yes. And even that does not have any guarantee." She looked at her watch. "Our best time will be in two hours, in the witching hour before the dark hour."

"Ah." Maggie nodded. "We're going voudon with this one?"

Lucia smiled. "And some other things. Are you out of practice with your Celtic magic?"

Now Maggie shivered. While she enjoyed certain magical perks, she preferred the intellectual detective work park of her job. "Maybe a little. But I guess it makes sense since Niniane is of that origin. I'm sure it will come back to me."

"Good. I have a place just outside the cemetery where I do my work. It's near enough to consecrated ground that we can go to it for protection, but still neutral enough for workings."

Maggie listened as Lucia outlined what she wanted to do. The woman was a genius, of that she had no doubt, but she also had a sense of foreboding.

She'd have to call in backup, and she knew just the guy for it.

WHEN PHILIPPE OPENED THE DOOR, he saw Maggie sat alone on the couch in the living room, her phone to her ear. Two mugs sat on the counter, and he wondered who had been there. That guy, maybe? A twist of jealousy joined the weight of the locket in his gut.

"Hi, Charlie?"

She *was* talking to another man! Philippe stepped back into the bedroom but kept the door cracked so he could hear. He clenched the doorknob with his left hand.

"Yes, I know." She laughed. "I didn't think I'd need your assistance again so soon, but we're planning a ritual tonight. Uh huh, at eleven."

Again? What had she been doing while he'd waited here for her? A dark well of anger opened in his gut near where the locket sat. The image of her kissing the guy popped into his mind, and the lock on the doorknob bit into his palm.

She told the man where they would be—somewhere near the cemetery. Of course. Could this situation get any creepier?

"Can you and your team be there for backup, just in case?" She lowered her voice, but Philippe still picked up what she said. "I've had warning that I can't trust him."

Now he held on so his knees wouldn't buckle. She didn't trust him? Her words speared him harder than when she'd said she wasn't interested in him, and the dark well of emotion turned into a geyser of resentment, again with the locket at its root. It didn't matter where his feelings came from. Hadn't they been through enough together?

He must have made some sort of noise because she glanced over her shoulder. Her eyes widened.

"Yes, thank you. Great, I'll see you later." She hung up. "Philippe?"

He couldn't back into the room and pretend to be asleep now, so he emerged. The cooler air of the living room brushed his face and hands, heated by anger. "You don't trust me?"

She stood and shoved her phone in her pocket. "Oh! I do, but I don't trust the locket and what it's doing to you."

"You don't believe I know my own mind?" He walked toward her and stopped just short of the couch. She didn't move away, but she eyed him warily. He tried to tell his fists to unclench.

"I know Niniane. Her magic is powerful. She was one of the most talented sorceresses I knew."

"And are you so helpless? You were her student. Surely she must have taught you some tricks."

She crossed her arms, and golden sparks flared behind her lenses, but she didn't remove them. "How do you know that? I'm giving you one chance to tell me before I truth-spell you."

"From a man at the airport. He said he's known you for a long time. He also said that you're the biggest obstacle to ridding yourself of the curse."

She shook her head. "He lied."

"Or are you lying to yourself?" He pointed at her, and confronting scratched the soul itch that had started when she'd rejected him. The resentment abated a little, but the anger still simmered. "Poor little Margaret running around saving everyone, but pushing them away if they get too close."

She inhaled sharply. "Now I know you're under its influence. This isn't like you."

He stuck his hands in the pockets of his pajamas. "How would you know? You've only known me for, what, two or three days? And who's Charlie? How long have you known him?"

She spoke quietly, her voice neutral. "An ally. And I just met him this afternoon."

"That's crap. You sounded like you've known him forever. He's the reason you don't want to even try to date me, isn't he? Not some bullshit curse."

She took off her glasses, but only to rub her eyes. "I'm not having this discussion again. You know my reasons."

At seeing her fatigue, Philippe's tension drained, and he had to grab the back of the couch when he swayed on his feet.

"You need to go back to bed," she told him. She walked around the couch to help him, but he waved her off.

"I can make it. Wake me up when it's time to go."

He stumbled into the bedroom and barely made it to the bed, where he collapsed into sleep.

Or thought he did. Now he stood across from the man in the gray suit in the middle of swirling storm clouds.

"How did it go?" he asked.

"Not well." Philippe sighed. "I really think it's futile."

"Well, one way to get someone like Maggie to attach to you is to let her rescue you." He tapped his temple. "Classic psychology."

Philippe crossed his arms—this place, wherever it was, had a damp chill. "I'm listening."

"Let me know where they'll be doing the ritual to rid you of the locket, and I'll create a diversion. Then she'll have to rescue you and care for you, and voila." He spread his hands. "She'll be yours and you hers."

Philippe opened his mouth, then shut it at a whisper of a suspicion at the back of his brain. "How do I know I can trust you?"

"I told you what you wanted to know about her, didn't I?" He smiled, but it wasn't pleasant.

"I don't have an exact location," Philippe said. He'd give a vague answer to get the guy off his back. "Just that it's somewhere near a cemetery."

"Ah, I know the place. The witch Lucia uses it often." He snapped his fingers, and Philippe awoke. He turned over, but the locket seemed to be forming a lump in his stomach, and he couldn't get comfortable. Someone who felt as exhausted as he did from the constant tug-of-war between his desires and his instincts should be able to go to sleep easily. He must have dozed off, because the next thing he became aware of was Maggie gently shaking his shoulder.

"Philippe? Wake up. It's time."

10

The cemetery wasn't far, but Maggie drove Philippe to it since he was weakening rapidly. After she settled him on a stone bench, Lucia handed her a rake. The two of them cleared the fallen leaves from a circular area about ten feet across in the middle of the clearing. Charlie and a small team arrived soon after and introduced themselves. Maggie braced herself for Philippe to be angry or jealous, but thankfully Philippe only shook Charlie's hand. Disturbingly, he seemed relieved to see Charlie. Maggie didn't think she'd revealed anything to Philippe—she didn't know the details of the ritual itself—but she also wasn't aware of how long he'd been eavesdropping on her conversation with Charlie.

Charlie and his team donned their helmets and melted into the woods around them to form a perimeter of protection. Maggie hoped that would be security enough. She would have preferred the cemetery itself, and she locked her awareness on the border of the consecrated ground so she'd know exactly where to drag Philippe should things go south. Lucia had just taken out the salt to purify it when a scratching sound made Maggie hold up one of her hands.

"What is it?" Philippe asked. She didn't blame him for being on high alert—they all were.

"Shhh." But she softened the hush with a smile. He nodded and appeared to relax. A wave of guilt washed over her—she'd spoken harshly to him, but before that, she'd allowed him to fall for her too hard. But she couldn't have done anything differently. It didn't matter—she couldn't focus on that now. Hopefully the noise was only some sort of woodland creature, but the sinking feeling in her stomach made her suspect otherwise.

"I heard something, too." Lucia frowned at the area they'd just raked. The sound happened again, this time from the other side of the clearing. Maggie held out a hand to pull Philippe to his feet, but the ground exploded between them. She fell back, spitting dry grass and soil, and landed on her ass as Philippe toppled off the bench. After she blinked the dirt from her eyes, she looked up to see Niniane towering over her. Her cousin lacked the aura power from their previous encounter—she must still be recovering from when Philippe shot her—but she had the energy of anger to strengthen her.

Maggie checked on the others as much as she could. The noise of a battle raging around the clearing told her Charlie and his men were busy, and Lucia used her long staff to fend off a couple of nightmare creatures with patchy fur and fangs.

Ugh, more were-bats.

"Well met, Cousin." Niniane lifted her chin. "You're looking well. Did your little organization take you back?"

Maggie tried to stagger to her feet, but Niniane held out a hand, and an invisible weight crushed her back. The waning light made something sparkle at Niniane's throat—the locket with Maggie's hair. Maggie groaned—she'd be vulnerable to whatever attack her cousin made unless she could somehow get it back.

"You're a fool to take me on as long as I have—whoops!" A

dark shoe swept Niniane off her feet, and she fell sideways. Philippe vaulted over her and helped Maggie to stand. He leaned on her, and she didn't object. If she held on to him, Niniane couldn't take him.

With supernatural-quick movements, Niniane stood. "That was a dirty trick, human. I'm looking forward to ripping my locket from you."

Maggie felt Philippe's fear through her fingers where they still held hands, and she tightened her grip. Could she access the power from Niniane's locket? Philippe's unfortunate feelings for her made it easy to follow the energy path down his arm, through his chest, and into his stomach, where Niniane's locket sat. The energy around it felt like black sludge, but Maggie grabbed it and raised her hand to block Niniane's next attempt to throw her back. Frustration twisted Niniane's face.

"I can easily have his hand cut off, you know." She gestured to one of the creatures Lucia fought, but when it turned, Lucia speared it with her staff between its greasy wings, and it disappeared.

"Use your eyes," Lucia called.

"Right. Good idea." Maggie ripped her lenses from her face and allowed her full Truth Seeker power to shine forth. A golden light diffused the air around them, and Maggie saw the truth in a vision.

Niniane stood on the shore of the lake and watched Avalon disappear into the mists for the last time as the sun set. She turned, frustration and hatred darkening her features, and a familiar-looking man in gray robes appeared by her side. He whispered something to her, and she smiled and nodded.

Maggie blinked back tears. She didn't need to know what the man had said to her cousin, who hadn't been cursed. It was always the same. She'd been twisted by the lust for the power she'd lost when the Arthurian golden age had ended, deceived as so many had been by the promises of the Gray Vampire. Did he still work with Niniane?

He hadn't appeared yet, so likely not. Maggie planted her feet and pointed at her cousin. "Niniane, I hereby ban—"

Now Maggie found herself on her stomach, having been tackled by one of Niniane's creatures. Philippe had tumbled to the ground with her and fought one-handed against the imp trying to get to his stomach with long, scalpel-sharp claws. He didn't let go of her, and Maggie kicked the creature off him. It cartwheeled through the clearing and crashed against the stone bench, lying dazed.

"Quick," she said. She and Philippe rose together, and blood streamed from the arm he'd been using to fend off the creature.

"Do what you need," he said, his face gray.

She squeezed his hand and turned to Niniane, who had circled around, knife in hand, trying to get a clear opportunity to finish Philippe.

"Niniane, I banish you," Maggie gasped with one more tug on the power of the locket in Philippe's stomach. Power rushed through both of them and in a stream toward Niniane. Maggie caught her breath when it tried to rebound at her, and she blocked it, bending back under its force. She focused on the weakness in Niniane's aura and gave one final push, picturing a dimension with no connection to the one where they fought, somewhere beyond the neighboring realms of Faerie and the Collective Unconscious. Somewhere Niniane couldn't make her way back from easily. With a shriek, Niniane disappeared, leaving Maggie's locket to tumble through space. Maggie darted forward, but with a metallic clink, it landed in the open hand of the imp, who took off with it.

Philippe fell to the ground and let go of Maggie. He curled into the fetal position, his arms clutched over his stomach.

"Go," he croaked. "I'm dying. They can't hurt me any more than I am."

Maggie knelt beside him. "You can hang on. You have to."

"I'll take care of him," Lucia assured her. "Go get your locket so they can't use it against you again."

Maggie hesitated. She felt the locket moving away, but Philippe had been so brave. "I can't just leave him."

"Go." He shoved at her leg.

She kissed his forehead. "Please don't die before I get back."

She followed the magic signature of her locket into the woods.

PHILIPPE'S LEFT ARM, the one he'd been using to ward off the creature-thing with the sharp claws, went cold, then numb.

"Can you help me?" he asked Lucia, who squatted beside him, her hands over his stomach.

She shook her head. "I'm sorry. You've lost too much blood, and that along with the power of the locket are killing you." She folded her jacket and put it under his head. He accepted her gesture of comfort even though it didn't help.

A shout from the side of the clearing startled them both, and Philippe tried to struggle to his elbows to see what was going on, but he couldn't and flopped back.

"What is it?"

"Niniane is gone, but some of the nightmare creatures remain. I fear Lieutenant MacKenzie and his men are outnumbered."

Of course they were. "Go and help them," he said. "I'll hang on for her. Don't let the nasty things get into town."

"You're a good man." She squeezed his shoulder, rose, and disappeared into the gathering gloom.

After Philippe had figured out he could sense ghosts, he'd wondered what it would be like to die. Would he become one? Did he want to live that afterlife, constantly missing what he'd had when he was alive? But then would death be like falling asleep, slipping into quiet darkness? Would it hurt? Would there be a bright light and angels?

The numbness had crept from his left arm to his shoulder, and when he looked at the limb, it seemed like it belonged to someone else, the fingers stiff and fingernails black, so he turned his gaze back up to the sky—blue velvet beyond a lattice of gnarled tree limbs. He thought he should be frightened, lying there all alone, but he found his emotions to be as numb as his arm, shoulder, and now back, like he gradually sank into the ground. Maybe that was dying, just sinking away.

A dark figure blocked his view of the sky.

"Move over, will you?" He asked. He would have laughed if he could have. "I'm dying with a view." He closed his eyes, expecting the final blow. Or claws in his stomach. Why couldn't that part of him have lost feeling? He could still sense the locket sitting in there like a rock. Or a tumor spewing poison.

"You don't have to, you know."

The clipped accent and supportive yet still condescending tone made Philippe drag his eyelids open. He saw gray pant legs, the creases perfect.

"You? I must be dead."

Something gently lifted him, then propped him up against one leg of the stone bench. The man came into view again, crouching on one knee. Philippe wondered if he would have to pay extra to get the dirt and mulch out of his suit.

"You're not, but you're almost there. What happened to your girl? Did you do what I said?"

Philippe nodded. "I held on as long as I could. And she did rescue me. But then I let her go so she could retrieve her locket." He blinked against the blurring of his vision. "It was the last thing I could do to protect her."

"Then you demonstrated true love. Would you like another chance? More time to help her figure out how to break her curse?"

Warmth spread through Philippe's limbs—that familiar tease of hope. "How?"

The man had never opened his mouth more than he absolutely had to in order to form his words, even when smiling. But now he grinned, showing fangs. Philippe attempted to scramble away, but his legs wouldn't obey him. He barely managed a foot twitch.

"Join me," the man said. "You will have forever."

Philippe's head slumped of its own accord, but his thoughts raced along on his final surge of adrenaline. If he were a dark creature, he could aid Maggie from the other side. And help her with her curse. They'd have forever.

"Yes." He barely formed the words with his lips, but the man heard. He yanked Philippe's head back and licked his neck.

"You've barely got any left," he complained. "But it will have to do for now."

"It will have to do for now," Philippe agreed. He closed his eyes at the sensation of the man's fangs entering his artery and thought about the times he'd said that phrase. In the hospital after he'd swallowed the locket and Maggie had told him about her curse. After she'd rejected his romantic dinner. Well, he'd have to do for now, at least for her.

"Now drink."

Philippe had seen enough vampire movies to know what he should do, but he resisted. Did he really want to do this? But the man pushed his wrist into Philippe's mouth, and after the first drop went down his throat, he couldn't resist.

The change started from his stomach out, burning his old self and leaving nothing but ash and despair and...

And Philippe clenched his hand around the locket that appeared in it. With his new senses and his old, he knew it was Niniane's. When he raised his head, the night had taken on a million more shades, like the difference between black and white and Technicolor. The sounds of the small creatures burrowing in the dirt under the concrete bench legs distracted him for a moment, but the man pulled Philippe's head back and looked into his eyes.

"Good. It worked. Now the locket?" He held out his hand.

"No." Philippe shook his head to emphasize his words. "It doesn't belong to you. Maggie needs it in case Niniane gets unbanished."

"You fool!" The man picked Philippe up by the throat and held him up so Philippe's feet dangled. "You're still new enough I can strangle you."

Crunching leaves heralded the arrival of two people to the clearing.

"Philippe!" Maggie had returned. He struggled to focus on her, but his vision blurred.

"Well met, Margaret," the vampire holding him said.

Then he arched his back and dropped Philippe, who landed in a crouch. The man clawed at his chest, where a narrow stake protruded. He fell to the side, revealing a helmeted and goggled policeman holding a crossbow, another wooden stake-arrow loaded, and trained on Philippe's heart.

11

After a series of twists, turns, and scrambles through the darkening woods, Maggie caught up with the imp and had him cornered against a large oak tree when he started to disappear back to his home dimension. She reached for him, but her hand passed through him.

"Dammit. I thought I had more time." She stepped back, and something whizzed past her. The imp rematerialized when a wooden stake impaled him on the tree, and she snatched the locket from its limp claws before turning to see who had helped her. She couldn't help a smile when she saw one of the cops standing there with a small crossbow.

"Thank you," she said.

Charlie removed his helmet. "And thank you. I've been hunting that one, but I couldn't get a clear shot until you cornered him." He walked over to her. "Are you okay?"

She put the locket on and sighed as the tension drained out of her at having it back on her person. Then guilt crashed over her when she remembered Philippe.

"Yes. No. Crap, Philippe is back there with Lucia. I need to get back to him."

"Your friend?" Charlie asked. "With the other locket?"

"Yes. He's gravely injured. I only hope he's held on." She could sense him, but barely, and then his energy changed. "Crap!" She broke into a run, and Charlie followed.

They burst into the clearing in time to see a vampire holding Philippe up by his neck. The gray vampire. Maggie groaned.

"Philippe!" She clenched her fists, but he turned and wagged a finger at her.

"Well met, Margaret."

Before she could reply, Charlie pulled a small stake from the quiver on his back, took aim, and fired. The vampire let Philippe go and toppled to the side before disappearing, but not into smoke and ash. Before he did, he smiled at Maggie, and she stepped back. She knew from experience that it would take more than a small stake to end him permanently—he was that powerful.

"Maggie." Philippe started toward them with a smile, showing a brand new set of fangs.

"No." Maggie put her hand over her mouth.

Charlie had reloaded and aimed at him, but Maggie put a hand on his arm.

"Don't shoot him."

"He's a new vamp. He's dangerous."

"No. No, he can't be." Not him. Not Philippe, who looked at her like he saw her as the girl she'd once been, not a Truth Seeker or associate of King Arthur, but just her. Maggie. She'd tried to push him away to protect him, but it hadn't worked. He'd been killed anyway, and now he'd be doomed.

Yes, the damn curse was in full effect.

"Look, Maggie, I've got the necklace." Philippe held out a hand to reveal Niniane's locket sparkling in his palm. "It came out when I..." He gestured to himself. "I changed."

Some of the tension in Maggie's stomach eased. At least she

wouldn't have to extract it from him. "Great, please give it to me." Maggie slowly walked forward but stopped when Philippe's nostrils flared.

Philippe took a step, his gaze locked on her neck. "Maggie, you smell amazing."

"It's because you're a vampire. A new one, and especially hungry." But she didn't move back. "Please don't come any closer. Just toss me the necklace."

She allowed herself a slight exhale when he stopped. Now a familiar expression crossed his face—confusion. "What's wrong? Why can't I come closer?"

"You're dangerous."

He looked at the necklace, then lobbed it to her. She grabbed it out of the air. When the cool metal met her palm, a tremor rippled through the ground. The part of her that had been attuned to the tunnels told her they'd closed with Niniane's last escape chance in her hands.

"Thank you."

"Now what?" He grinned, revealing his new fangs. "I can help you with your curse now. You and me. We have all the time in the world."

"No." She shook her head. "It's already too late." She gestured to his changed form, and thick tears threatened to choke her. "You've already been doomed."

"It's never too late!"

The air vibrated with the anger in his voice and energy, and Charlie moved to her side.

"Can it be reversed?" Charlie asked. "Since it just happened?"

"No." Maggie struggled to breathe around her grief. She hadn't meant for this to happen. "We need to contain him, but"—she lowered the crossbow, which he'd raised—"not kill him. I can't have his death on my hands any more than it is."

Philippe watched them, his lips twisted into a snarl. "I'm so hungry." He looked down, and when he lifted his head again, the ring around his irises glowed red. "And you smell delicious."

Maggie didn't have time to react when he lunged at her, but the twang of the crossbow indicated Charlie had. The stake caught Philippe in the shoulder, and he staggered back, his swipe barely missing her. A glowing golden lasso closed around him, and he disappeared. The lasso also vanished, but the man holding it didn't, and he stepped out of the shadows.

"Merlin," Maggie said, pressing a hand over her pounding heart. "Have you been there the whole time?"

"Long enough." Merlin shook his head, but he grinned. "You do like to cut things close. And who is this?"

"Lieutenant Charles Allen MacKenzie." The two men nodded to each other with familiarity. "But you knew that."

Merlin nodded. "Lieutenant MacKenzie."

Charlie inclined his head. "Sir Merlin."

Maggie recalled their previous conversation. "He's one of the humans you've recruited as part of your experiment. That explains how he knew who I am."

"Correct. And he's performed admirably. You can expect to work with him in the future."

Good. So she'd remain a Truth Seeker. As for further contact with Charlie... She'd sort her feelings out about that later. "What did you do with Philippe? Please tell me you didn't kill him."

"Unfortunately I don't have cause to execute or hold him indefinitely since he hasn't killed anyone yet, but we can at least get him through the transition. Then I'll release him somewhere he won't do much, if any, harm."

She didn't know where that would be, but she didn't ask. Hopefully he would find a nice lady vampire to take his mind off her. And maybe he would agree to help their side at some point. Eventually. After he'd gotten over her and gained control over his new urges and powers. And forgiven her, if that was possible.

"We need all the allies and help we can get," Merlin said as though he'd read her mind. He may well have. She was too exhausted to block her thoughts. "And you need to rest. Signs and portents are pointing to unrest in the Collective Unconscious, and Zeus has been missing for long periods of time. I'm going to need you again sooner rather than later."

"And me?" Charlie asked.

"Likely." And with that, Merlin disappeared.

"Wow." Maggie looked around. Night had descended fully, and the sounds of battle had given way to the stirrings of the nocturnal wildlife. "Where did everyone go?"

"The others are on creature cleanup," Charlie said. "Lucia said she'd help. My job is to get you home safe. Do you want to get something to eat? There's a Waffle House nearby."

Maggie looked up at him. Another young man. Another handsome face. Another guy she'd try not to put in danger.

"I need some time to myself after all that." It wasn't a lie.

"Understood." Disappointment flickered over his face, but he didn't pout. "It's hard to lose a colleague."

She nodded. "Exactly. Especially like that. I shouldn't have left him."

"Don't second guess yourself." He clapped her on the shoulder like she was one of the guys. Maybe that's all she could be, but this time the notion didn't satisfy her. "You couldn't have known a vamp was waiting to grab him."

"No, but I should have suspected." She rubbed her eyes. "But thanks. I appreciate your support." Her words sounded hollow.

They walked toward town through the cemetery. Charlie didn't holster his weapon until they were well on consecrated ground.

Then he asked, "What did he mean, now you have all the time in the world?"

"I don't know." But she suspected. Could her curse be broken? That little glimmer of hope made her smile. "But I aim to find out sooner rather than later."

ABOUT THE AUTHOR

Cecilia Dominic wrote her first story when she was two years old and has always had a much more interesting life inside her head than outside of it. She became a clinical psychologist because she's fascinated by people and their stories, but she couldn't stop writing fiction. The first draft of her dissertation, while not fiction, was still criticized by her major professor for being written in too entertaining a style. She made it through graduate school and got her PhD, started her own practice, and by day, she helps people cure their insomnia without using medication. By night, she blogs about wine and writes fiction she hopes will keep her readers turning the pages all night. Yes, she recognizes the conflict of interest between her two careers, so she writes and blogs under a pen name. She lives in Atlanta, Georgia with one husband and two cats, which, she's been told, is a good number of each. She also enjoys putting her psychological expertise to good use helping other authors through her Characters on the Couch blog post series.

Find Cecilia Online

Mailing   List: https://www.
subscribepage.com/CDbackofbook

Website: www.ceciliadominic.com

Facebook: www.facebook.com/CeciliaDominicAuthor

Goodreads: https://www.goodreads.com/au-
thor/show/5011217.Cecilia_Dominic

Instagram: https://instagram.com/randomoenophile/

Cecilia's books available everywhere e-books are sold. Look for paperbacks online and in select brick-and-mortar stores.

If you'd like to get a peek at the first full-length book in the Dream Weavers and Truth Seekers series *Tangled Dreams*, please continue reading for an excerpt.

TANGLED DREAMS SNEAK PEEK

Please enjoy this preview of *Tangled Dreams,* the first full-length book and next tale in the Dream Weavers and Truth-Seekers series...

"My baby! Someone stole my baby!"

The cry jolted through Audrey, and she dropped her sausage and egg biscuit. It landed with a splat on the plate and fell apart, but she didn't notice, having half-risen to search for the flurry of activity that should accompany that kind of cry. But the only curious glances she saw were directed her way. She sank back to her seat, trembling with unspent adrenaline.

"Did the sandwich try to escape?" J.J. wiped a bit of mustard from his close-cropped beard. "Or did you just see that cop you've been coffee-stalking?"

"No." Audrey glared at him and attempted to suck in a couple of belly breaths. "Didn't you hear that? Someone just got kidnapped."

"The only thing I heard was your breakfast hitting the paper and falling apart." He gestured to the table between them.

Audrey looked down. He was right. The sausage hung over

the open bottom half like a panting tongue, and the scrambled egg pieces had scattered in a half-hearted bid for freedom. She retrieved the top half of the biscuit from its precarious position at the edge of her plate, but she had to clench her hands in her lap to stop their shaking. She snuck glances to either side. How did he not hear the panic-stricken call for help? Or anyone else?

"That's what I get for asking them to hold the cheese," she attempted to joke.

J.J. raised an eyebrow. "Told you it'd be better with it all melted together. You should listen to your brother."

She only half-listened to him yet, her attention on the nearby moms with small kids, but no one indicated they'd heard or made the cry.

"I know I heard it." With mostly steady hands, she did her best to reassemble her breakfast, but her fingers still felt weak. Was this the first step to madness?

"You're edgy today. Did you get enough sleep?"

She snapped her gaze back to him. Something tickled the back of her mind in response to his question before it was swallowed up by the tension that always overtook her when he tried to 'brother' her. He was her editor, not her brother, for Pete's sake! Okay, he was her brother, but they were here to discuss her next day's assignment, so she tried to keep things professional. But she had to answer.

"Yes, Kyle gave me a sample of something last night. Some drug that's been getting a lot of press." She cringed, anticipating his reaction.

As expected, J.J. rolled his eyes. He was nice and predictable like that. "Just because the media likes it, doesn't mean it's good for you."

Instead of getting into the same old argument, Audrey took a bite of her biscuit, but her heart still beat in her throat, and a piece of sausage stuck. She coughed, and J.J. reached across the table and thumped her back.

"Maybe you should take the rest of that home," he suggested. "You're not doing so hot with thinking and eating at the same time."

"You're probably right." With a sigh, she wrapped up the rest of the breakfast sandwich and stuck it in the paper bag with the apple she hadn't touched. She hated it when he was right, but there was no point in choking on a bite due to her imagination, which had been going strong since the night before with vivid dreams she could only remember in flashes. She'd woken feeling like she hardly slept.

J.J. stood, as did she, and another glance around the coffee shop revealed her favorite cop, who walked into the coffee shop. His uniform hugged his broad shoulders, and she knew from previous sidelong glances that he had a nice, tight ass to go with them. The best part for her was his gray eyes – bedroom eyes, her mother would have called them – that stood out against his olive skin and wavy dark hair. Somehow his appearance calmed the deep inside part of her that still trembled with the sense that something was very wrong.

"What are you smiling at?" J.J. turned around. "Oh. Is that him?" he asked in a stage whisper.

"Shut up before I punch you," Audrey said through clenched teeth behind her smile.

The policeman must have heard them because he turned toward them and cocked his head when he saw J.J. like he thought he looked familiar. Then his gaze met Audrey's, and he smiled.

Audrey returned the grin and waved before following J.J., who'd become suddenly eager to go out into the bright autumn sunshine.

"Do you know him?" Audrey asked once the door closed behind them. "He looked like he recognized you."

"Nah, you know I've got one of those familiar-looking faces." But J.J. didn't slow his pace. "You could talk to him, you know. Actually say hi, give him your number."

Although the idea thrilled her, Audrey shook her head. "And what? Ruin the fantasy?" She practically trotted to keep up with him. She'd forgotten how his skinny pants obscured how long his legs were. "Besides, haven't you forgotten something important?" She poked him on the biceps with each word. "I. Have. A. Boyfriend."

"I wouldn't know," J.J. told her. "Considering I never see you with him or hear of you hanging out with him."

She couldn't argue with that. Instead, she reminded him, her smile gone, "You know my rule: no dating cops. Too much of a chance they won't come home."

Finally J.J. slowed and looked at her. She guessed they both had the same sadness in their green eyes. "Like Dad."

Why did thinking about that horrible night still make her throat swell with tears that should have run out by now? "Right, like him."

J.J. gave her that mixed sympathy with a look that said, "Your reasoning is a flimsy excuse," but he only asked, "Do you want a ride home?"

The cry came from Audrey's right: "My baby!" She turned so quickly she almost lost her balance. Two women sat on a restaurant patio with brightly-colored tables and chairs. Between them, they had five children, all young, a laughing, squirming, tumbling mess. One of the moms held out her arms to a blonde cherub, who toddled around in a diaper and pink t-shirt.

"There's my baby," she cooed. "What a big girl you are, walking all by yourself."

Audrey blinked to clear the buzzing sound from her ears, and the sense of wrongness returned. "Yeah, a ride would be good so I'd get home faster. I need to lie down before Kyle gets off. I'm hearing things."

J.J.'s cupid's bow lips curled. "It's probably your biological clock."

She punched J.J. in the arm. "Just because you don't want kids doesn't mean I'm going to pick up the slack for you."

He smiled, and the corners of his eyes crinkled. "But really, how are things going with Kyle? Do you actually have a date with him this afternoon, or does he just hook you up with sleep drugs? That's a dealer, not a boyfriend."

"No," she sighed. "I'm hoping he'll have time for coffee. Since he's on his sleep rotation, he's got to be back tonight to observe study hookup, but he said he might stop by after they're done rounding at the hospital."

J.J. used the keychain remote to unlock the car, then opened her door for her. "I don't like how he treats you."

Audrey slid on to the soft leather and waited before he got into the driver's seat before saying, "Not everyone was raised a gentleman like you. Besides, he's a medical resident. Things will get better once he goes on fellowship."

"Uh huh." J.J. pulled the car out of the square and turned right. Audrey wondered how to continue the conversation, but decided not to. J.J. liked to be overprotective.

But what if he's right?

Audrey rolled down the window to let the air in to cool her cheeks and distract her from her doubts. The Bartlett pear trees, red at the top, yellow in the middle, and green on the bottom, ruffled in the breeze, which carried hints of chilly nights to come. She took a deep breath, savoring the autumn smells: dried leaves, wood smoke... *Wood smoke? It's warm to be running a fireplace.* The aroma disappeared.

The car carried her through the neighborhood and past a small park, where someone had dug up the bed in the middle to plant a flat of pansies. The flowers sat by an abandoned set of tools, and the red clay stood out against the still-green grass, a gash in the earth.

Audrey's vision tilted, and dizziness made her grab the door handle to anchor herself. She'd seen something like that recently. The memory tickled at the back of her mind. *That's where I heard the cry the first time.* But it had all been a dream...

"My baby!" A distraught woman in tan robes screamed and looked into a pit of fire. Hands held her back from jumping in.

Audrey blinked, and the scene faded. It had only been a dream, a vivid dream. So why did her stomach knot just thinking about it?

"Audrey? Audrey!" J.J. shook her shoulder, and she realized they'd pulled up in front of her duplex.

"Sorry, daydreaming." *Or day-nightmaring.*

He didn't release her. "You look like you're coming down with something. Maybe you should just take the night off from everything, even Kyle."

"I'll think about it." She hoped he didn't see how she had to clutch at the door to keep her balance when she got out of the car. He didn't say anything, so perhaps not. She waved as he drove away.

"Someone took my baby! My baby girl!"

The cry reverberated through Audrey's head and faded into throbbing pain. She'd managed to distract herself after her weird morning. But now that she had time to take a nap, she couldn't get the sound of sobbing out of her head. Listening to music hadn't blocked it. Talk radio only made it worse - no surprise there. She rolled over and clutched her pillow to her face, willing away the sensation that someone stood just out of view and watched her attempts to sleep.

Why won't this dream go away? She hit the pillow in frustration and opened her eyes. The clock said three fifty-four. Kyle would arrive soon for coffee, which she had brewed. Maybe. If the afternoon didactics hadn't run long. If he didn't get caught up in conversation with his fellow medical students. And if the sleep lab wasn't totally booked.

"If, if, if. And I have a major headache, so I'm totally justified in eating all the cake. Right, Athena?"

Athena the calico cat meowed, and Audrey scratched her behind the ears. After deciding a change of scenery may help, she and the cat both curled up on the sofa, and the cat's purring had almost lulled Audrey to sleep when she got a text from J.J.

"Have a bad feeling about tomorrow's article research. Don't go to Bistro Moderne."

"Now you're just being weird," Audrey texted back. *"No one's blown my cover yet."*

"Trust me on this one. There are more secrets than just yours."

"Huh, I wonder if this has anything to do with the cop at Java Lemur." She once again wracked her brain for any connection her decade-older stepbrother could have with a cop, but came up with nothing but the vague sense she didn't know J.J. as well as she thought.

Athena pushed her head under Audrey's hand.

"I'm talking to you a lot these days, huh, Athena? I need a normal man in my life, not a paranoid, overprotective stepbrother or a distant boyfriend."

As if on cue, her phone buzzed with a text from Kyle: *"Can't make it. Too much work. C U tomorrow?"*

Audrey hesitated before replying. Two could play at this game. But she hated to be the jealous girlfriend. Medical school was intense, but there was a major payoff at the end of all the training. She'd get through it with him, not make it more difficult.

With a sigh, she replied, *"Don't work too hard. Tomorrow's tight."*

"Will call u." Then a kissy-face emoji.

Would he? Or would it be another day of excuses? She silenced her phone and flopped on her back. *And that's why I need sleeping pills, even if they do cause weird dreams. Maybe I'll dream up a solution for what to do with my screwed-up life.*

Go to www.ceciliadominic.com or your favorite retailer for more information on Tangled Dreams or to grab your copy today!

PERCHANCE TO DREAM SNEAK PEEK

Please enjoy this preview of *Perchance to Dream*, the first story in the Dream Weavers and Truth-Seekers series...

Emma stood in the doorway and squinted into the peach-colored light that had appeared without warning to disrupt her sleep. She put a hand out to steady herself and snatched it back when she touched the rough-hewn wooden door frame. The walls of the room seemed to have just been put up, the beige dry wall barely set. Sawdust and wooden curls littered the plywood floor. The sounds of others murmuring and moving about reached her ears. She backed up until her back touched the wall and...

Emma woke, her hands still clenched. She lay in bed, awakened by her husband bumping into her. He rolled away when she gently shoved him back. She snuggled into the flannel sheets, twitched her shoulder blades until they were comfortable, and closed her eyes. With a sigh, she slept...

...and found herself back in the room, standing in the door.

What kind of hella-vivid dream was this? The sweet-sharp smell of the wood filled her nose, but at least the sawdust on the rough plywood floor didn't make her sneeze. Normally in her dreams she had difficulty moving, but this was no different than her waking life. She walked through the room and found a door on the other side, also unfinished, and a hallway. More rooms lined the hall, some with only wooden framing, others further along but not complete.

Voices carried down the hall, lively conversations and laughter. This comforted and frightened her simultaneously. Where were these people? She heard footsteps behind her and turned around...

...and woke again to the sound of a car alarm going off outside the window.

"Just effing steal it already," Greg mumbled into a snore. Emma nudged him.

"Turn over," she said. He did. She didn't want to go back to sleep, but drowsiness overtook her...

She found herself in the same doorframe in the same room off the same hall. *What the hell?* She knew that in the past, she had continued a dream upon awakening once, but twice was unheard of.

"Oh, there you are."

She spun around and found herself face to face with a person, mid-twenties, who seemed to be simultaneously gender-less and dual gendered. Slender and with dark hair, they wore a simple tunic and pants outfit of navy blue. The person's large brown eyes captivated her, as they seemed to belong to someone far older than the chronological age of the rest of the being.

"Who are you?"

"Adrian." The person's voice gave no clue as to gender, as it could be a low-pitched female's or tenor male's.

"I'm Emma."

"I know. Lucy told me about you."

"Lucy?"

"The Madam Lucia? The psychic you spoke with today? Yesterday, actually."

Emma shook her head. She knew that had been a bad idea, but, really, what could she have done?

She'd gone to Target for packing supplies and was headed back on Highway 29 when her cell phone rang. Lightning overhead had made the reception poor, but she could hear the voice of Grace, her mother-in-law.

"Hello, Emma," Grace snapped. "Is this a bad time?"

The corners of Emma's mouth tightened. "Yes, actually."

"Well, I won't keep you but a second. Is my son there?"

"I'm driving right now. In the rain." *And Greg's at work, as you well know.*

"I just wanted to ask him if this would be a good weekend for us to come see the house. We're so excited for you."

Of course she'd called to ask him, not them. "We're excited, too, but we need to see how the move goes before we can make any plans. As it stands now, we're planning on having a house-warming party at the end of the month."

Emma swerved to miss a puddle and earned a honk from a driver whose lane she'd invaded.

"Sure, but don't you want us to come up before that? To help out?"

Not really. "I really appreciate the offer, but I'm sure we'll be fine."

"Well, I'll just talk to Greg and see what he says. Go on with your errands, and we'll see you soon."

Emma sighed and tossed the telephone into the passenger

seat. She knew how it would all play out. Grace would call Greg and guilt trip him for not inviting them up before the house-warming—*"But honey, don't you want to spend time with us?"*—and then they would come and pick and nag—*"I don't mean to tell you how to set up your kitchen, but I've had my glasses in the cabinet by the sink, and it's just worked out so well for me for twenty years"*—and do it so sweetly that protesting would make her, Emma, look like the bitchy, ungrateful daughter-in-law.

She hadn't seen the glass bottle until she rolled over it and heard the pop under the right rear tire. The car groaned and pulled to the right. She drove into the first parking lot, put her forehead on the steering wheel, and cried in frustration.

A tap on her window startled her, and she looked up to see a tall, dark-skinned woman dressed in blue jeans and a black linen top embroidered with flowers in red metallic thread. The woman wore her hair long and in braids, and it faded from copper-colored at her crown to blonde at the bottom. She looked at Emma with friendly black eyes.

"You are having a rough day, yes?" she asked in a lilting accent.

Emma looked up and saw that her car was one of two parked in front of a small whitewashed frame house with purple curtains in the windows. The sign over the door said, "Madame Lucia, Palm Reading $5."

"Yes," she sniffled.

"Come inside, and you can call a tow truck from there."

Emma straightened. Did everyone think she was completely helpless? "Thanks, but I can change a tire."

"Then let me help you." Madame Lucia, Emma presumed, held a large red and white golf umbrella. She helped Emma change the tire—an unwieldy process since it involved unloading and reloading the trunk. By the end of it, Emma felt doubly grateful she'd had someone to hold an umbrella over her.

"Um, thanks," Emma said once they'd completed the task. The woman inclined her head. "Do you have anywhere I could wash my hands?" Emma held up her grease- and dirt-stained fingers.

"Of course. I have a bathroom inside. You may clean up there."

When Emma emerged from the bathroom, Madame Lucia had an old-fashioned tea set on the small coffee table in the living room. Emma thought of excuses she could make to leave, but her growling stomach gave her away.

"This is all really very nice," she said, "but..."

"But nothing. It is a slow afternoon, and I had the kettle on for tea anyway."

Emma sat on the couch. "Thank you."

She sipped her tea in awkward silence and nibbled at a scone. "These are very good," she finally said.

"Thank you. I made them myself."

"Do you usually serve them to, ah, clients?"

Lucia shook her head. "Oh, no. Only to, how shall I say it? Equals? Colleagues?"

Emma put the scone back on the delicate china plate. "What do you mean?"

"Your palm, when you showed me, said that you have some sort of perception beyond that of normal people."

"No, nothing out of the ordinary here." At least nothing helpful.

"Then please forgive me. I can make mistakes sometimes."

Tea ended amiably enough when an actual customer drove into the parking lot. Emma hoped it wasn't anyone she knew as she ducked out, got in her car, and drove home.

"I didn't really consult her," Emma said to Adrian. "It just happened that I ended up in her parking lot. I had a blowout."

Adrian shrugged. "Regardless of what brought you to her, it was meant to be that you saw her."

Emma wasn't going to argue. "What is this place?"

"A new extension of the dream world, the CU."

"CU?"

"Collective Unconscious."

"Oh." She'd heard something about that in her intro to psychology course. "So the repository of dreams?"

"Yes, the archetypes that visit people's dreams." Adrian walked down the hall, so Emma followed. "This is a new phase to allow those with talent to have easy access to the place." They lowered their voice. "They're trying to improve customer service."

Emma peeked in rooms. Some were completely finished and decorated in widely ranging styles from a seventeenth-century boudoir to a twentieth-century New York penthouse. Some lacked even drywall.

"I don't have any talent."

Another shrug. "You must have some if you were able to get here."

Emma decided this was a very interesting dream and that she might as well play along. "Like what?"

"Clairvoyance, psychic, ESP, whatever you want to call it. Strong intuition beyond that of 'normal' human beings."

"I tried to tell Lucia—there's nothing special about me. I must have gotten let in by accident."

Adrian gave her a patient *you must be a dolt* smile. "You were invited, and you accepted. You may not realize that you accepted, but you did. And now you have a room."

Obviously arguing wouldn't make a difference. "Why are they all the same size and shape?"

"It's how they're doing all the new developments these days. There are also some lovely amenities, like free access to most of the Manor parties."

"Manor parties?"

"The dwelling places of those who live here."

Emma shook her head. "This is all very confusing. Where are we going?"

Adrian didn't reply but continued to walk, so Emma followed. They passed down one long, straight hallway that seemed to have no end in sight.

"Where are the windows?" Emma finally asked to break the silence.

"Oh, they'll be put in last," Adrian replied with a wave of one hand. "That way they won't interfere with ideal object placement."

"The windows will be cut out after the rooms are done? That will be a mess."

"No." Adrian gave Emma a quizzical look. "They'll be hung."

"I don't get it. How can you look out a hung window?"

Adrian turned to her with the same infuriatingly patient expression. "The same way you look out any other kind."

"But won't there be a wall behind them? What will they overlook?"

"Whatever the resident wishes."

"Oh, so they're more like screens?"

"They'll have screens if you like. Especially if you decide to look over scenery where things may fly in."

A faint beeping floated through the air and grew louder. Adrian halted, cocked their head, and looked at Emma with gray eyes. Before Emma could ask why they had changed color, Adrian said, "That will be your alarm, I think. Bother, I had wanted to take you to the manor. Ah, well, another night, then."

"Right."

Adrian and the scene melted away, and Emma rolled over to turn off the alarm and turn on the bedside lamp. She sat up and swung her feet over the side of the bed. For a moment, the light caught something that fell from her foot to the floor. She picked it up—a curl of wood.

"What's that, hon?" Greg asked.

"I'm not entirely sure." Emma crushed it in her palm, then threw it in the small wastebasket by her side of the bed. "I had a very interesting dream this morning..."

Wait, what's happening to Emma? Is the Collective Unconscious a real place? Can dreams really come true, and if so, would you want them to?

*If you'd like to read **Perchance to Dream** for free and get updates on when new Cecilia Dominic novels will be released, please go to https://www.subscribepage.com/CDbackofbook to sign up for my newsletter. I hate spam and promise to keep your information safe!*

CPSIA information can be obtained
at www.ICGtesting.com
Printed in the USA
JSHW010139280120
3839JS00001B/43